Diviner's Nemesis I
- Avenger -

Maggie Shaw

Diviner's Nemesis I
- Avenger -

Maggie Shaw

eregendal.com

Also by the Author

The Vision and Beyond
(After the Night of Fires)

First published in the United Kingdom in 2019
eregendal.com, Crewe, Cheshire
Printed in the United Kingdom by Lulu.com

ISBN 978-1-9996071-2-8 (paperback)

Contents

INTRODUCTION
and
ACKNOWLEDGEMENTS

Diviner's Nemesis is a story of revenge, set against a backdrop of occultism and the paranormal in late 1970s London. When Liz Kirkland marries archaeologist Alec Graham after a whirlwind romance, she little realises the part she will play in his attempts to bring his arch enemy Jonathan Keast to justice. The death of Alec's friend, the actor Andrew Ferry, leads her into the dangerous world of the psychic organisation P.S.I. and the demonic powers at its heart. Will she destroy the evil there before it can destroy her? The unfolding story explores prescience, faith, betrayal, forgiveness and redemption as it explores the clash of two male egos through the experiences of the woman they sacrifice to their rivalry.

The story of Liz Kirkland was originally written in a series of five episodes in the 1970s. Parts 1 and 2 are contained in this volume: *Diviner's Nemesis 1: Avenger.* Parts 3, 4 and 5 are contained in *Diviner's Nemesis 2: Retribution.* The evolution of the story over time has been influenced by the wisdom and advice of many people, most significantly Bob Thomson. I would also like to thank Helen Lamb and Roy Butler for their assistance with the manuscript. Any faults in the work are my own alone.

The Biblical passages quoted are from the New Revised Standard Version and the King James Version of the Holy Bible. The Tarot sequences are based on the system outlined in the book *The Tarot Speaks* by Richard Gardner (Rigel Press Ltd 1971).

Prologue

The Ace of Swords

Interpretation: unanticipated danger

threat, death, suicide

Prologue

The room was dark. Heavy brocade curtains screened the windows and the doors, shutting out all the world beyond. The only light came from an oil lamp suspended over the velvet-covered round table, creating a small area of focus in the draped maroons and shadow blacks.

He had come because he knew her reputation as a diviner had been proven many times. She faced him across the table, all too aware of his reputation as a dangerous man.

Her henna-decorated hands glided through the air around the crystal ball between them, her blood-red nails glinting with reflected flame. She had to concentrate, to ignore his threatening presence, to look through the crystal ball to the reality that lay beyond.

At first she saw nothing, just the sparks of elementals dancing across her perception as they looked for souls to leech. She felt the walls of his reserve, shielding his psyche from her probing, preventing her from giving him an easy reading created of his own hopes and fears. He was forcing her to go much deeper, into her true arts. His fierce dark eyes compelled her to go on, to dive through the mists to whatever lay beyond.

The first image came as a flash, and was gone. She had seen him, lying in the back of a car on a rain-washed street, his spirit curling away like smoke into the ether. When she tried to conjure up the image again, only darkness prevailed, lit by the dancing sparks of elementals.

Her hands stilled, cupped round the crystal ball, as she waited for her vision to clear again. Clouds slowly covered the darkness, swirling in light greys around a woman with the face of a painted doll. She blinked, and that too had gone. Nothing she tried could bring the image back again.

'What have you seen?'

She feared telling him but knew she could not leave the visions unsaid.

'I saw a beautiful woman, a painted doll. And you had lost all you hold dear.'

He took a deep breath. This was the third warning. He knew he had to act, to trace the painted woman and prevent her from making the auguries come true.

'Who is she?'

She shook her head. Her hands released the crystal ball. The henna-decorated fingers draped a cover over the table, declaring the session closed.

He dropped some money on the cloth and left.

Part 1

Card 6: The Lovers

Interpretation: true love

a choice between love and ambition

1 : 1

'That's him!' cried Bethany Broome. She ran out into the High Street to catch the man, her copper hair streaming and her blue wool suit flapping in the cool breeze.

Liz Kirkland watched her friend from the doorway of the Antiquarian Bookshop, well used to Bethany's impulsiveness. She leaned against the window frame, a relaxed young woman with long black curly hair, wearing an embroidered blouse and folk-weave skirt. Along the street a tall well-dressed dark-haired man stepped into a taxi which quickly drove him away. Without thinking Bethany flagged down another taxi and set off in classic pursuit.

'What's that about, Liz?' asked portly Harry Simms, looking up from a case of books he had bought at auction. He wiped the dust off his glasses with the hem of his beige work-coat.

Liz made way for a customer to enter the shop and re-joined Harry at the box of books they were sorting, as the new customer immersed himself in the paperback shelves.

'Isn't it obvious?' she said, a mischievous glint in her green eyes. 'That's the man Bethany thinks sold Mike the drugs he got done for having in his pocket that couldn't possibly have got there if it hadn't been a plant.'

'Do I detect a slight hint of disbelief there, Miss Kirkland?' Harry said.

'Not for Bethany; but her boyfriend is quite another matter. That's why her father keeps trying to buy him off, only Mike hears the sums go up and holds out for even more.'

'Isn't thirty a little old for that?'

'Maybe, but twenty-one recurring isn't.'

Liz pulled a small red volume out of the box and found she

was holding a book on her wanted list: *Astronomica* by Manilius in the original Latin with an English translation.

'Uncle Harry, can I keep this one and offset its price against my wages?'

He checked the book and agreed on a nominal amount.

'Your fortune telling is subsidising the shop, Liz. Shouldn't it be the other way around? It might be cheaper if you worked in the betting shop next door. But there again, perhaps not.'

The customer interrupted them to pay for three paperback westerns. He was a curly-headed young cockney, and Liz saw him pick up one of her business cards from the counter as Harry opened the till for change.

She waited for the customer to leave before asking, 'Is that a regular?'

'No - first time here, though I have seen him in the High Street from time to time. Another client for you, perhaps?'

'I hope it's his wife or sister – I dread his type. It's awful reading the cheapest Tarot spread with only the odd grunt in response.'

Heavy footsteps pounded down the rickety stairs from the apartment above, heralding the arrival of Harry's son Guy, a blond Adonis in neglected sweatshirt and jeans. His striking face was flushed with exciting news.

'We've got the go-ahead! Our first really big order: ten thousand brochures for the trophy company up the road, with an option for more!'

Harry and Liz congratulated Guy, knowing what the order meant for his young business. His life revolved completely around the Print Workshop, as Liz had discovered the year before when she had gone out with him for three months. After she had realised he was far more in love with his press than with her, she had discreetly relinquished him to her new flat mate, student art teacher Frances Fitzwarren. Fran had long been impressed with Guy's daydreams and did not mind in the least being placed second to his struggling business.

As Guy was enthusiastically reaching the end of his second version of the good news, Bethany walked back into the bookshop, dishevelled and disappointed. She flopped tiredly down on a bentwood chair by the till.

'I lost him!'

'Who, Mike?' Guy asked.

'If only,' Liz chipped in.

'No, the man who slipped Mike the drugs he got done for carrying that he said couldn't possibly have been there,' Bethany replied. 'I was going to give him a piece of my mind.'

'Probably just as well you missed him then,' Guy said: 'I can just see the headlines: *Drug Baron arrested for Wimbledon shooting – "I couldn't stand being nagged to death," he confessed.'*

'Oh, shut up!' Bethany protested, slapping him lightly on the shoulder.

'Don't fret, Bethany,' Harry assured: 'Justice will catch up with him soon enough.'

1 : 2

Liz arrived home from work that evening to find Fran in the kitchen preparing their evening meal. Fran was as poor a cook as Liz and only ventured into the kitchen because they had arranged to cook evening meals for each other to ensure they both regularly ate something more substantial than beans on toast.

'What is it?' Liz asked from the hallway of their flat, not recognising the powerful aroma.

'Frozen lasagne with some extra toppings. Guy asked me to try out the recipe for his *New Woman* page,' Fran replied.

She placed the lasagne back in the oven and emerged from the steaming kitchen, a striking young woman who dressed with style and distinction despite her low budget. Her fine straight chestnut hair was cut with Egyptian angularity in harmony with the severe lines of her dark brown dress, and in contrast to the soft gentle form of her slender freckled face. After gaining an art and design degree Fran had continued her studies by training to teach because the student hours at her college gave her plenty of spare time to work with Guy at the Print Workshop. It also meant she was often home to take Liz's phone messages. With a bright smile she handed over Liz's open appointments diary.

'You have a client this evening, Liz: one Mr Graham. I tried to persuade him to let you call on him but he insisted it wasn't safe.'

'Oh, a loony! Just what I need.'

'He sounded educated and well off with it so at least you should get a good run for his money. Starters at seven thirty for the whole works and an all evening job.'

'I don't know how you do it, Fran: my business has trebled since you started answering the phone. Just stay in with me if he'll let you and I'll buy you fish and chips for tea tomorrow.'

'Done!'

Fran returned to the kitchen to serve up their dinner. The lasagne proved far more palatable than her usual burnt offerings. They raced through the meal to give themselves enough time to tidy the lounge before the client arrived.

The doorbell rang precisely on seven thirty. They peered through the lace-curtained window to get some idea of what to expect. A large black Lincoln Continental four-door limousine had parked outside. At the wheel sat the curly-haired young man who had picked up Liz's card in the bookshop that morning. The client was out of view in the shadows of the porch. Fran hurried out to the hall to bring him in while Liz arranged herself on the sofa with her Tarot cards on the coffee table before her. She settled her thoughts to prepare for the reading ahead.

'Liz, this is Mr Alec Graham,' Fran introduced, ushering her client in. He was a short slender man of about forty, elegantly dressed in a well-tailored suit of midnight blue. His dark hair and neatly trimmed beard were flecked with a few strands of silver. His eyes were compelling and forceful, dominating a distinctive face which Liz recognised with the prompt of his name. She stood up and offered him her hand in welcome.

'Dr Graham, I am honoured. And also a little surprised that an archaeologist of your reputation should visit a fortune teller.'

His eyes scanned her in quick appraisal. She was small and slender, a fragile creature clothed in rustic simplicity with untidy long black hair and flashing green eyes. How much was image, he wondered, warning himself to guard against the temptation of liking her.

'Very impressive, Miss Kirkland. You have done your homework well,' he said, ignoring her offered hand.

She waved away the ignored handshake in a gesture inviting him to take a seat.

'I did no homework, Dr Graham. I read your paper on Minoan symbolism, in last autumn's Archaeological Society journal. You made some interesting points. Would you like some tea?'

'No, thank you.'

He wordlessly instructed Fran with a pointed glance to leave their company. She calculated that Liz would be safe with him and acquiesced, making an excuse to return to the kitchen. When she had gone, he sat down in the tired armchair on Liz's right, his full attention on the fortuneteller as she shuffled her Tarot cards.

'How did you come across that article, Miss Kirkland?'

'One doesn't work in a place like the Antiquarian Bookshop without being given some access to publications on one's favourite subjects.'

'You are interested in Minoan symbolism?' His disbelief was plain.

'Not just Minoan. The psychic and the occult use symbols to express things beyond words and to describe complicated things in simple terms. By studying mankind's collective symbolism, I can understand more of the images I receive in divination and trance.'

He turned away in scorn, and by chance his eyes fell on the small red book she had brought home with her. He picked it up in surprise.

'Manilius? Then you are serious about this?'

'Oh, yes: my principal interest is in the spiritual realm - my fortune telling is just a way to practise the use of symbolism and pay some of my bills. And I sense you have no personal interest in fortune telling. You are not here tonight to have your cards read or your horoscope cast. But you are here with a problem - no, you are here to have a question answered.'

'How much of that is your psychic ability, and how much have I given away?' he asked, resisting the temptation of letting her impress him.

She sensed his inner conflict between scepticism and belief and challenged it with a dramatic flourish. Adroitly, she spread the Tarot pack face up across the coffee table and selected the Empress, card three from the Major Arcana. He looked with uncommitted interest at the crudely drawn picture of a robed woman seated on a throne surrounded by a sheaf of ripe corn, a river and a wood.

'This is Juno. She has great influence over you, but she is only Hera in a younger guise, so I am being told,' she said.

He knew at once that she was talking about his adoptive mother and demanded suspiciously, 'Told by whom?'

She observed him thoughtfully for a moment, sensing his discomfort that she might see through his reserve.

'Are you sure you want me to continue, Dr Graham, or would you rather ask me your question and go? I wouldn't be offended: only my bank manager would find cause to complain.'

He laughed despite himself, caught out by her unexpected remark.

'No, let us continue. I would like to see how you use your

knowledge of symbolism to play the parlour game of Tarot.'

She realised his remark was deliberately provocative and did not rise to the bait. Instead, she handed him the full deck of cards and asked him to shuffle them.

'Please ask your question as you shuffle the cards. If you would prefer not to tell me at this stage, I can give you a general reading, which you would have to apply to your circumstances.'

'I have no intention of giving you any clues,' he replied, and handed back the shuffled deck.

She laid out the top fifteen cards face up on the coffee table in three rows of five. After reflecting on the pattern, she explained what she saw.

'This row of five represents your past. Death, coupled with the four of Wands, tells of an inheritance which brought, by the seven of Wands, a change of work concerning wrong-doers or deceivers – the Devil – for which, by the Ace of Pentacles, you have had to make a business trip recently.'

'That is true enough. Carry on.'

'The middle row of five represents your present situation. A deceiver – the Magician – has become a false friend – the inverted four of Cups – and you are risking a lot through him – the six of Swords. From the nine of Wands and the Enchantress, you are being advised about the matter by a powerful woman.'

Liz paused, her finger on the last card in the middle row as she waited for his response.

'Part of that is true enough' he admitted. 'But I don't think any powerful women know about it.'

'Her power is not necessarily worldly command or monetary wealth. She is a woman you may not realise is powerful, because her strength lies in her ability to wield men whichever way she wants without their realising. Shall I move on to the future?'

'I see. Yes.'

'The Hanged Man, representing an unconventional or painful truth, results in the Lightning Struck Tower, implying that your old way of life will change dramatically as the deceptions strip themselves, releasing you from the negative situation which surrounds you. The nine of Pentacles suggests you will end up paying out money for it in a form of self-promotion. And the three of Cups implies the final result, a love affair or an engagement.'

'Huh! Happy families!'

'If it wasn't there, I wouldn't say it. From bottom to top, column one, the death of a relative attracted a deceiver about whom you may learn a disturbing truth. Column two, the inheritance and its implications made the deceiver a false friend, but in the future that should change dramatically when his true colours are revealed. Column three, it is in your work that you are taking the risks, which should pay off with care. Column four, the deceivers that your work is concerned with, are the subject of the powerful woman's advice, and it is because of her you may spend money on self-promotion. Column five, it is because of your recent business trip that you are involved with the powerful woman, with whom you are likely to have an affair or get engaged.'

'Interesting.'

After some thought he slid a photograph out of his inside jacket pocket.

'That is enough Tarot. Have you seen this man before?'

She recognized the person in the photo as the man Bethany had chased after that morning. With a brief nod she handed the picture back, disliking the psychic shadow surrounding his image.

'Yes, and you are right not to trust him, Doctor. He is connected with something that disturbs you, I sense: someone dear in lilies. But he was not the culprit - he is some distance away in the linking of hands.'

'What do you mean?'

'The number of people connecting him with the dear one who died: they never met.'

Her words brought back his memories of his brother's tragic death. He wondered how she could be so accurate about his understanding of the events when she knew nothing about him. Reason still nagged that this was a sham, that her words could be interpreted in any one of a hundred ways. But emotionally he felt naked in her presence and was both fearful of her and attracted to her because of that.

'Where did you meet this man?' he asked.

'I haven't actually met him. I just saw him once, this lunchtime, as my friend Bethany Broome chased him up the High Street. They disappeared in separate taxis. Why does he have the Greek letter psi on his tie?'

Dr Graham feigned surprise at this and checked the photo to make sure the logo could be seen.

'So he has. You were overheard saying he is suspected of drug trafficking.'

'Are you a part-time policeman?' she demanded, unsure of the confused image she was now perceiving of him. When the confusion dissolved, she saw the person in lilies again, the image tinged red with his burning anger.

'No, just someone who does not like drug traffickers!' he spat.

'Bethany claims this man slipped her boyfriend Mike a packet of drugs just before Mike was arrested for possession. So when she saw him in the High Street she went chasing off after him to give him a piece of her mind.'

'Why didn't she simply go to the police?'

'Because she is besotted with Mike, and sadly he is about as straight as a nine pound note. Her father has tried to buy him off, but he keeps hearing the price go up so he's sitting tight.'

'Her father isn't by any chance Stanley Broome, the sculptor, is he? That rambling place not far from me, by the common?'

'The very same. Not that I know him that well. Bethany and I have been friends since schooldays. So no, I would not go to the police either – that's her decision to make. Anyhow, I have only hearsay evidence.'

He felt disconcerted to find his questions being answered before he had asked them.

'What made you say something as specific as that?' he asked.

She smiled gently at him, pitying this reserved stranger who felt so compelled to fence words with her. All too easily she saw through his persona to his psychic image of a sword. He was a classic example of the Tarot symbol of intellectualism: quick-witted but cold and merciless. For all his elegance he was a dangerous man. She answered him tactically.

'Nothing made me say that. It just seemed the most appropriate thing to say.'

He patronised her with an indulgent smile for her defensive response and was surprised to see her blush. She had an air of vulnerability which he sensed was born of her innate truthfulness. He found it refreshing after the falseness of the world he had left behind outside her door. Here where he had least expected it, he had stumbled across a woman who interested him. He wanted to see her again, away from her professional setting, and quickly thought up a ruse to achieve that.

'There is no need to be so cautious, Miss Kirkland. I promise you I intend no argument. Would you be willing to help me prove the involvement of this man in the photo with the drug trade?'

'Only if he is definitely involved already, or has a chance to prove his innocence if not. I won't frame him.'

'I wouldn't expect you to do that!'

She refused to let his impatience daunt her.

'Then how do you intend to make him betray himself?'

'He is already my acquaintance. You and I could be friends: with a visit to a beautician and a hairdresser and a good clothes shop you should be able to make a reasonably convincing girlfriend for me. I will invite you and Miss Broome over for dinner with Pierre and myself. During the evening you can take him to one side and proposition him for some drugs.'

'Do I really look that bad?' she laughed, making light of his unintentional insults to make him gently aware of them. She asked more seriously, 'Is this man psychic?'

'I don't know. Possibly, when he has that logo on his tie.'

'The Greek letter psi, Neptune's trident? If there is the slightest chance he is, don't ask Bethany along for he will sense the instant he sees her that it's a trap. Bethany may be a good actress but she doesn't know how to hide herself psychically, and she doesn't like him at all. My flatmate Fran would be a safer choice. She knows nothing, which would be both her protection and yours.'

'How would you know then to ask him for drugs?'

'I could tell him I know Mike, which is true.'

'Then you will do it? Strictly business terms, of course: I will pay you for all your time plus your expenses, and for a suitable outfit for your friend. Yes, perhaps her sense of style would appeal to his taste.'

Liz marvelled at his effortless ability to be insulting but would not let that prevent her from enjoying an unusual assignment.

'Yes, I will do it, Dr Graham - I'll enjoy spending a week in beauty parlours at your expense,' she agreed with a teasing smile. 'But for it to be a success you must learn to protect yourself psychically too, and that will be as hard for you as it will be for me to look chic.'

He returned her smile with a roguish look close enough to a suggestive leer to make her blush again.

'There is no time like the present, Miss Kirkland - I did book you for the whole evening.'

'Fine,' she countered. 'How good are you at enveloping your psychic body in a blue-edged halo of white light?'

1 : 3

'That must have been some impression you made on Dr Graham last Friday,' Fran declared to Liz as the archaeologist's Lincoln took them to his detached commonside house Briarbank for dinner a week later.

'He made quite an impression on me too!' Liz replied with guarded levity, nodding at the curly-headed chauffeur Theo to warn Fran to guard her tongue.

Fran's face set in a sour expression. She did not like deference to wealth although she liked the idea of being wealthy. For Liz's sake she was tactful enough to refrain from comment while they were out, but Liz knew she would speak her mind when they were alone together later on.

'At least I can say I've worn a Sabatina dress,' Fran said, feeling good and looking dramatic in a copper and cream creation in chiffon, waisted and full.

Beside Fran Liz felt unable to compete with a woman eight years her junior, though to less critical eyes she looked more polished and elegant than her younger companion. With her long black hair drawn back from her immaculately made-up face into a tumultuous tumble of curls, she looked stunning in a white dress of classic simplicity and design which fitted her like a glove.

The limousine turned into a driveway through high hedges opposite the common and drew up outside Briarbank, a large chocolate-box Tudor-style house set in well-kept grounds. The heavy oak front door opened and Dr Alec Graham came out to greet his guests. He was wearing an unfashionable slate grey velvet suit which Liz thought made him look very distinguished, while Fran thought he looked fussy and effeminate.

'Liz, my dear!' he greeted warmly, taking both her hands as he swiftly appraised her appearance and judged she had got the balance just right.

Behind him, Pierre Eve appeared in the doorway, turning on his Gallic charm to compliment the two ladies for their beauty. Alec introduced them all.

'This is Pierre, who is staying with me at Briarbank for a few days. Pierre, these are my friends Liz and Fran.' His intonation as he said Liz's name suggested a much closer relationship.

Pierre hid a momentary reaction of dismayed surprise during the introductions, which Liz picked up. As they all walked inside chatting, he deliberately focused his charm on Fran.

Alec was a skilful conversationalist as host and ably led the evening in the direction he wanted. He conveyed a deepening attachment to Liz with subtle understatement, which she returned in like manner but with caution, fearing that her attachment could become all too real. Pierre observed their performances while entertaining Fran with his gallant asides and well-informed comments about art. Fran relaxed in the warmth of his gentle French accent and forgot her more extreme opinions for a while to experience the evening for itself.

Alec's housekeeper had produced a traditional crown roast as the centrepiece for dinner, allowing Alec the pleasure of impressing his two female guests with his household cuisine as well as the decor. The traditional meal contrasted with its setting in the distinctive dining room, where satin oak furniture was set off against light grey walls and rough slate-grey floor tiles. Alec loved to appear different and to incur approval, Liz noted, but she sensed he preferred not to draw comment at all than to be criticised.

As they sampled an apple chiffon dessert, Fran took the opportunity of Alec and Pierre's debate about an international news item, to whisper an aside to Liz.

'Pierre's been asking questions about you. What should I say?'

'In what way?'

'It was after you refused to drink the wine of his birthplace, and he took it as an insult.'

Liz smiled to reassure her. Alec had saved the situation by explaining to Pierre that Liz did not drink alcohol for religious reasons.

'If he asks again, just tell him the truth.'

'What was that you were saying, Liz dear?' Alec enquired to stop their whispering and take back control of their conversation.

'I said "the truth", Alec,' Liz firmly replied: 'The truth is that neither of you can walk through the Foreign Minister's mind so neither of you can be more than speculative - you can't resolve the debate one way or the other. Gamblers anticipate results too, and look what happens to many of them.'

'Elizabeth, is that not a little strong, when you can?' Pierre said. She perceived his amiable protest to be more pointed than it seemed on the surface and wondered why he had called her by her formal name.

'My apologies,' she said, with a sidelong glance to see whether Alec had understood the undercurrents in Pierre's comment.

Alec smiled indulgently at her, hearing only her readiness to back down for him. She sensed his image in her third eye once again as linked to the goddess Juno and suspected he was measuring her up in terms of his mother. The thought pleased her. Despite his contradictions she felt drawn to him, as if it were their fate to have met. Reality returned to remind her theirs was a purely business relationship.

She looked up at Pierre and was taken aback to find him staring at her. He had been trying to walk through her mind. She sent him a psychic warning shot to keep out and turned her attention back to Alec who had started a less controversial topic of conversation.

After dinner Liz found herself alone with Pierre in the cream and maroon brocade lounge while Alec stood with Fran

28

in the panelled hall, telling her the history of a painting which had caught her attention there. Pierre opened the cocktail cabinet in the lounge and offered to pour drinks for them all. He set out two port glasses and two brandy goblets and turned abruptly to look at Liz with an expression which she felt went right through her.

'I have seen you before, Elizabeth, haven't I, in the doorway of a bookshop.'

'You have. Did you sell him the drugs?'

He turned back to the cabinet and poured out the drinks, caught out by her directness, which he covered by taking affront.

'What a question to ask! I should throw this drink over you for such an accusation.'

He handed her a glass of port. She set the glass back down on the cocktail cabinet.

'You misunderstand me, Pierre. For religious reasons I do not drink alcohol. That does not mean that one cannot take coke.'

'Ah, a Daughter of the Wheel,' he said with a smile, referring to a non-conformist sect which had sprung up in alternative circles. 'That is different. How much?'

'Enough for my personal use. It's only recreation for me. I expect good quality, but I am willing to pay for it.'

'I shall not disappoint you. A hundred when you next visit. I will do the rest.'

Pierre smoothly returned to pouring the drinks as Alec and Fran joined them from the hall. Liz stepped back from him, feeling like a conspirator.

'Thank you, Pierre, but I would rather drink coke. Alec, would you mind if I ask Mrs B for more coffee?'

'Of course not, Liz dear,' he replied, and went with her to covertly show her the way to the kitchen.

The housekeeper, ample Mrs Buxton, was still busy in her kitchen overalls, finishing the washing up with her tall, lean son

Sam whom Alec employed as a handyman. Liz complimented her on the evening meal. She glowed bashfully as she bustled over to the hotplate to pour a fresh cup of coffee from the bubbling percolator.

'You can speak freely here, Liz,' Alec said. 'Have you approached him yet?'

A feline smile settled on her face. 'Oh, yes, Dr Graham; and you are quite right to be concerned about Pierre Eve, as your tape will show. He recognised me from last week, which gave me a good place to start. The deal is a hundred pounds for some good quality coke. He mistakenly believes me to be a Daughter of the Wheel, an impression I made no attempt to discourage as it seemed to satisfy him about why I don't drink but do fix. Is that enough for you?'

'You've done well. We must finish it tomorrow, to give him as little time as possible to find out the truth about you. I'll give you a surprise invitation to a concert tomorrow night.'

'Fine, but say no more or it won't be a surprise. And watch yourself - you've been forgetting to protect yourself psychically this evening, and Pierre does have psychic vision. He already senses our relationship is not as we claim, so all the "my dear"s in the world won't convince him of our whirlwind romance.'

'Your coffee, Miss Elizabeth,' the housekeeper said with a kindly look of approval over her spectacles as she handed her a steaming cup.

Liz and Alec returned to the lounge to find Pierre and Fran having a lively discussion about art education. They quickly drew them in to take sides. The light-hearted debate continued so late that Liz and Fran had to threaten to play Cinderella to bring the pleasant evening to a close. Alec gave Liz his surprise invitation in the hall as he placed her wrap about her shoulders before she left.

'By the way, Liz, I managed to pick up two concert tickets for tomorrow night: Walton and Elgar. Interested?'

'Try to keep me away! Elgar is my favourite composer, as

you well know. But what about Pierre? Won't you be offended at being left out?'

'Alas, I have a meeting tomorrow evening, Elizabeth. When I see you both off before you go, you will see my envy: even I prefer Elgar to oratory.'

'That is settled then, Liz. Theo will collect you at five for tea here before we go, and we can snatch a theatre supper somewhere after.'

He walked Liz and Fran out to the waiting Lincoln in the cool night air and waved as Theo drove them away. The limousine swept out of the shingle drive onto the commonside road. Fran settled back on the leather seat with a scowl.

'I hope I don't meet Pierre again, Liz. You know he's a merchant of death.'

Liz looked at her face by the intermittent light of the streetlamps passed by the car.

'I had my suspicions. What made you so sure?'

'He offered me some angel dust. I pleaded ignorance, of course, just like when he asked me how big your habit was. Maybe I led him on a bit about being an international artist and a woman of the world, but it doesn't automatically follow I'm a pin head. And where he got the line you're a pin head, I don't know.'

'That's simple. I asked him for a coke instead of port. He took it the wrong way.'

Fran looked at her in astonishment and gave a tipsy laugh. The joke appeared to amuse her for the rest of the short journey, but her smiles stopped the moment they closed their front door on the chauffeur-driven limousine and the unusual evening. Liz flopped tiredly down in an armchair and kicked off her high-heeled shoes in relief. Fran threw herself across the sofa and let her shoes fall to the floor.

'You know, Liz, I was going to warn you what a sell out you'd be making if you teamed up with Alec. Then I thought I was wrong because I enjoyed the luxury and Pierre's conversation. But then I found Pierre's a pusher and I thought, that just goes to show you only get that sort of wealth trading in other people's lives. What can we do about him?'

'If you're worried, tell Guy. I'm going to have to tell Alec.'

'No, I can't: Guy thought I was home studying tonight. And you shouldn't tell on a man's best buddy, which they must be when they were arguing about the Foreign Minister without any malice after. And you really set the cherry on that cake with your bit about anticipating results. They were furious till Alec realised how heated they'd got and began to laugh.'

'He laughed because he thought I sounded like his mother.'

'Really? That must be why her in the kitchen liked you so much. Is she the handyman's mum?'

'Yes: they live in the flat above the garage.'

Liz sighed and stretched her tired body, knowing she should go to bed but too excited after the unusual evening to want it to end. She would have liked to spend the night telling Fran how wonderful she thought Alec was, but she knew her flatmate did not have such a positive opinion of him and restrained herself.

'It's a whole different world to ours, Fran. This was meant to be just a job, just for a day... But now I find I really like Alec, for Alec, not for his trappings. Despite all he has his life is so empty. Emotionally, spiritually; physically too, I suspect for he doesn't unbend. I'd love to help him find the reason and take it away, to help him open the doors onto what he's missing. But all his chattels get in the way, and I don't even know if I'll see him again after tomorrow.'

'Is that cad playing with your affections that much? For all those loving words of his, he's only turned you into his painted doll to throw you away?'

'No, it's not like that, Fran. But for the moment I just can't tell you any more.'

Fran nodded with confident understanding of the situation, resolved to settle that uncertainty for her friend as soon as possible.

1 : 4

Liz returned to Briarbank next day resplendent in emerald green which brought out the colour of her green eyes. Behind her immaculate make-up and polished finish she felt apprehensive. Alec detected her unease as he took her coat and asked her what was wrong.

'I don't know, Alec: someone's been walking over my grave all day. Where's Pierre?'

'Uptown at another meeting he was suddenly summoned to attend this morning. He should be back soon. I think he suspects.'

'No matter. You already have him - he touted for business with Fran too last night.'

'Theo mentioned she said something to that effect. He also said Pierre quizzed her about you.'

They strolled through to the lounge where the housekeeper had left a well-laden tea trolley with plates of neatly cut sandwiches and an assortment of home-baked cakes. Alec noted the spread as he handed Liz a plate and a serviette.

'I think Mrs B likes you. I am finding I quite like you too.'

'Ah, but is it me you like or your mother?'

He turned away indignantly, stung by the jibe.

'I'm sorry,' she apologised at once, embarrassed to have caused such unexpected hurt through her teasing.

She made time to think by pouring them both tea. When she had worked out what to say next, she spoke again.

'I find this so difficult, Alec, because we don't meet on equal terms. I've been unprofessional enough to become emotionally involved and I don't know how to handle it. As soon as I've completed your commission, I should go.'

He appreciated her attempt not to take advantage of the situation.

'But why? We work so well together. And I can tell from the

33

way you talk about symbolism that we have an interest in common, though we might sometimes disagree about the substance. And you don't know how refreshing it is for me to find a beautiful young woman so genuinely enthusiastic about my work. And I was the one who turned you into such a beauty.'

His declaration took her aback. 'I think God had a hand in it too,' she protested, recalling Fran's comment about a painted doll and thinking, God made the doll and Alec provided the paint.

'Yes, I've been hearing all about your work with the chapel,' he continued unabashed: 'What an interesting man Father Jeremy Kingston is. He tells me you're a great help with his youth group.'

'You have been doing your homework on me, haven't you! And that's why Theo came into Uncle Harry's bookshop last week, wasn't it - doing the homework on Pierre.'

As she spoke her sixth sense warned her that if she became any more involved with Alec, he would convert her into his property and entrap her as the latest showpiece among all his other possessions.

'Unfortunately, one has to in my position. But the more I learn about you, the more special you prove to be. We don't have to end our relationship when this sordid business is over: if you are agreeable, we can continue to see each other.'

Because she was already falling in love with him, she ignored her inner warning and accepted his excuse.

'Agree? Of course, Alec - my only fear was that we would part for good tonight.'

Still her inner voice nagged, warning her that despite their sincerity they seemed to be speaking from the script of some dated romantic film. She ignored the thought that perhaps one of them was acting and saw only the pleasure in his face reflecting the joy in her own.

'Excellent - that is settled, then! Tomorrow I shall take you on a tour of my world. We shall phone Mother and Philip to come over to meet you - I'm sure Mother will be as delighted with you as

I am. And we shall have a proper dinner party where you can meet my real friends. And you can help me sort out my work and classify my papers.'

She looked thoughtfully at him, wondering whether she would be permitted to object to any of his plans.

'That sounds good, Alec. Just bear in mind I will still be working too - I do have to support myself,' she ventured.

Her hint of resistance took him aback. He reminded himself that though he knew a lot about her, they had only met a week ago. Despite her already having changed a lot for him, he should still expect her occasional lack of co-operation as she got to know him more and gradually left her independence behind. Fortunately for him she did not read the thoughts behind his smile as he offered her a sandwich.

A short while later they heard Pierre's Peugeot car turning into the drive.

'Do you have the envelope, Liz?'

'Yes, Theo gave it to me in the car. I've addressed it to Pierre as he told me to. But we hardly need that now, do we.'

'Please go through with it. Before I act I have to be sure.'

Behind his voice they heard the front door open and Pierre announce that he had returned. Alec called back that he was with Liz in the lounge. Pierre strolled in with a friendly greeting and dropped elegantly onto the sofa.

'What a day!' he exclaimed; 'And more tonight. The Chairman *est un fou*! The Chairman is angry; but he is angry about nothing. Ah, Elizabeth, never involve yourself in society politics. Alec, I have some figures for you.'

Pierre reached inside his jacket. Alec tensed automatically, expecting a weapon, but relaxed again when all he pulled out was a report. He accepted the papers from him and leafed through them.

'Does he know about these, Pierre?'

'*Non*. But they demonstrate the reverse to what you thought: these accounts are perfectly legitimate. *Mais pardon*, Elizabeth:

you will forgive us our small piece of business, yes?'

'Of course. Would you like some tea?'

Alec felt the time was right to spring his trap and stood.

'If you will excuse me a moment, Pierre, I need to make a quick phone call,' he said, and left the lounge.

Once he had gone, Pierre rose from his seat and joined Liz at the tea trolley. He pressed close to her as she poured him a cup.

'Why did you lie to me, Elizabeth Kirkland?' he whispered, uncharacteristic venom distorting his gently accented voice.

She faltered but stood her ground with him. 'Strong words, M. Eve, and I am not in the habit of lying.'

He tugged at the gold chain around her neck, pulling out the gold crucifix she always wore, with a tug to emphasise its significance before letting it drop onto her dress. She firmly thrust a cup and saucer into his hand, her manner frosty.

'Your tea, M. Eve. Don't call me a liar when you simply made a wrong assumption based on insufficient evidence. I'll get your money.'

She sat down on the sofa and opened her handbag. When she handed him the long brown envelope Theo had given her, his mouth curled into a sneer. He counted the notes it contained and slipped the money away inside his jacket.

'The merchandise is already in your bag,' he said. 'I look forward to doing business with you again. You will need to here. I know you believe this is just for today but time will prove you wrong. You will regret that.'

'Really? I think you are being very presumptuous, M. Eve.'

She checked her bag, found the small packet of white powder in the purse pocket, and called out to Alec.

He walked in at once. Pierre realised he must have been waiting at the lounge door and knew that despite his sixth sense they had trapped him.

'Alec, I think your friend has been using your house to distribute cocaine,' Liz said: 'See, he has just slipped this into my

36

bag without my knowledge.'

Alec took the packet from Liz and asked Pierre, 'Is this true?'

'What do you think!' Pierre scoffed: 'You hardly know her. Of course she doesn't drink - your new *cherie* is a drug addict!'

Liz blanched, for his statement was more accurate than she thought he could know. Alec ignored her response, having learned of that episode in her life while checking out her background during the past week.

'Whether that is true or not, it is irrelevant, Pierre,' he said coldly: 'I have suspected you for some time. It was I who asked Liz to proposition you, and I who gave Liz the envelope to give you. Must I prove it with the denominations and the numbers of the notes? Shall I play back the tape?'

He opened the sideboard door to reveal a recording cassette machine. With a flick of some switches he played back part of the conversation in the lounge while he had been out of the room. Pierre stepped back warily towards the door. Alec turned off the tape and angrily swung round to face him.

'You knew exactly how I feel about drugs, and why; yet still you played this trick in my house!' he shouted: 'Get out!'

'But Alec, this is not as it seems,' Pierre protested with a look of hurt innocence which only inflamed Alec's anger the more.

'Get out while you still can, Pierre. And while you're running, I'll send these figures of yours straight back to their source with my calling card. So you'd better not stop running, had you!'

Horror distorted Pierre's face. He pleaded with Alec to reconsider. Alec's intensely bitter refusal warned Liz that somewhere therein lay the cause of the resentment so damaging to his life.

'No, M. Eve, I only give you the same chance you give your customers. Now get out, before I have to get Sam to throw you out!'

Pierre left. He knew Alec's reputation in his circles and did not delay even to pack his bag. The Peugeot flew out of the drive onto the commonside road, spraying shingle across the immaculate lawns.

1 : 5

Liz felt a shadow descend over the lounge after Pierre Eve had left. The time had arrived for her to make the confession she knew she must, and she feared that so much honesty so soon would destroy the relationship she wished to encourage.

'I apologise for all that unpleasantness, Liz, but it is all over now,' Alec said confidently, unaware of her dilemma: 'Now we can begin a more conventional relationship.'

'I didn't mind the unpleasantness - if not for Pierre Eve I would not have met you.'

He appreciated her flattery but was concerned to see her face remain pensive and wondered whether she was already having second thoughts. She sipped her tea and gave him an uncertain smile.

'Before we go any further, Alec, there is something I must tell you. Pierre was right when he said I'm an addict. About twelve years ago my doctor prescribed me some tablets to help me cope with things, and I had a terrible job getting off them again. I was drinking far too much too, and it caused me a lot of problems. That's why I don't drink or do drugs now, and why I go to Father Jay's chapel - there's a group there for that sort of thing.'

She put down her teacup and stood up.

'And now I expect you want me to go.'

'No, why should I?' he said dismissively, already aware of her background and her recovery. 'Twenty years ago I used to smoke. It was considered all right then, but it isn't now and I don't smoke now. You don't take your pills and things now. Oh, if only all our guilty secrets were that simple.'

'Then you don't mind?'

'Of course not. It makes me respect you more. You've fought your demons and won. And you chose to tell me, even though you found it very difficult...'

A commotion outside interrupted him. The housekeeper opened the front door to see what was causing the disturbance and was pushed aside by four visitors. Her cry for help brought Sam and Theo running to her side from either end of the house, but not before Fran had led Bethany and their boyfriends Guy and Mike into the lounge.

'Where's Pierre Eve?' Bethany demanded angrily.

'He has just left, for the continent. Who are you?' Alec asked in return, his cool manner betrayed by the angry glint in his eyes.

Liz hastily introduced her friends, wishing the ground would open up to swallow them before they did any more damage to her position.

'That crap don't wash with us, mister. We know he's here, and we want him,' Mike blustered, acting the big man while oblivious to the danger he faced with Alec in front and Sam and Theo behind. The cocky manner of the flashy young man showed Alec at once why Liz disliked him and why Bethany's father had tried to pay him off to stop seeing his daughter.

'Young man, remember you are a visitor in my house. If you cannot improve your manners, you will be escorted off my premises. Eve was obliged to leave here suddenly because he abused my hospitality. I would have no qualms about ordering my men to eject you too.'

Mike glanced back and faltered to see the stamp of the men who stood ready behind him. He waved his hands in a gesture of submission which displeased Fran.

'But what about Liz?' she demanded.

Alec saw Guy's eyes dart across to Liz with a protective expression and guessed their common past. In acute embarrassment Liz started to plead a reason to escape the scene. Alec interrupted, ordering her to stay so abruptly that she sat down at once.

'Liz, there's nothing we'll say that you can't hear,' Fran promised her and turned to Alec. 'Dr Graham, why are you leading Liz on? She told me last night she doesn't even know whether she'll see you again after tonight. That's no way to conduct a relationship, under threat.'

'Miss Fitzwarren, your loyalty to your friend is admirable, but the way we conduct our relationship is none of your business. Go back to your paints and your proofs where you can do less harm.'

Fran looked from Alec's smouldering anger to Liz's embarrassment and suddenly realized the difficulties her jealousy was causing her friend.

'I'm sorry, Liz,' she apologised and turned to leave.

On Alec's nod Sam and Theo escorted Guy and Mike out after her. When Bethany tried to follow Alec called her back.

'Miss Broome, I would have expected you to know better,' he warned.

She studied him thoughtfully, her concern for Liz making her consider her response. She could see how much Liz was already taken with this vain and arrogant man and had not liked the harshness of his command when he had ordered Liz to stay.

'Dr Graham, I'm sorry my friends and I have come across as rude and insensitive. These things were of great concern to us and we thought our only option was to call on you. Obviously we were wrong,' she apologised.

'If you want to repair the damage, I'd like to meet your father. Can you arrange that for me?'

'I'll do my best, Dr Graham. But I don't see much of him now, not since he stopped throwing Mother through the window and started on me instead.'

She nodded curtly to him, squeezed Liz's hand in fond farewell, and followed her friends out of the house. Alec watched from the lounge window as they departed in Bethany's maroon Volvo 246 saloon. Once the drive was empty, he spun round on Liz.

'I take a very dim view of the way you have broadcast our relationship to all and sundry, Liz, a very dim view indeed. Your friends knew less than half the tale and have jumped to completely the wrong conclusion.'

Liz risked a protest, but her protest was defensive.

'Alec, don't forget Fran was with me last night. She saw our expressions across the table and heard what we said. That was the evidence which made her draw her own conclusion, that you are leading me on. When I tried to explain after we got home last night, I made the mistake of letting slip I might not see you again after today. I'm sorry. What else can I say? I can only promise to take care not to discuss our relationship with others again without your permission.'

Her ready submission mollified him. He crossed the room to take her hands and draw her up out of her seat.

'There is no need to say any more. Come on, my unpredictable Liz. Let's put this behind us and go and enjoy some Elgar together.'

She stood up at his bidding, smiling again because he smiled, happy again because the black clouds had been dispelled.

1 : 6

Over the next three days, Alec hijacked Liz's life. One trip at a time, one day at a time, he took her on a whirlwind tour of his world and his interests. Each day her own plans somehow fell through and she followed his instead, without really thinking about it. When apart from him, she looked forward to seeing him again. When with him, they laughed and joked and made memories: strolling by the Thames at dusk, discussing symbols on exhibits in the British Museum, laughing at the clowning street performers at Leicester Square.

They returned to Briarbank late Thursday afternoon,

enthusiastically discussing the exhibition they had been to see. Alec picked up the post and asked Mrs B for tea in the lounge. As he leafed through the bundle of envelopes, his face changed. He put down the pile of post on the coffee table and sat on the sofa to study a monochrome postcard of Beirut that had just arrived.

'What's up, Alec?' Liz asked.

He sighed.

'Liz, tomorrow I must return to the Lebanon, to see a mutual friend. I don't want to go, but I have to.'

'Why? What's wrong?'

'Nothing's wrong. It's just business.'

She knew he was lying. Her face fell.

'How long will you be away for?'

'No more than a week.'

Mrs B brought in the pot of earl grey tea he had ordered. Liz took the tray from her and poured out two cups. She handed one to Alec before sitting in an armchair to drink the other.

He looked thoughtfully at her, trying and discarding several openings for what he wanted to say next.

'Things can happen suddenly, can't they,' he ventured at length.

'That's certainly true,' she replied lightly: 'I've only known you ten days, but it feels like we've known each other forever.'

He smiled. 'Yes, I feel that way too. And when I'm with you, I feel so alive.' He paused again.

'Liz, before I go tomorrow, there is something I must ask you. I had wanted to choose a better moment, but that's not possible... Liz, will you marry me?'

The cup in her hand rattled violently. She stared at him, open-mouthed, at a loss for something to say. He saw her shocked expression and realised he had sprung the question too soon.

'I can see it has come as a surprise. I didn't intend that at all. But when we're together, I feel a different man. I don't want to lose you. And I really don't want to go, but I must.'

'Perhaps it is just as well that you are going,' she ventured. 'I think, maybe you've been dazzled. Yes, it's fun being with you, and I've loved the things we've been doing together today. But maybe once you're in the Lebanon you'll realise I'm not half what you imagine me to be.'

'No, I'm not dazzled: I know more than enough about you to know that. You are one of the few people I feel I can trust. You don't know how precious that is to me.'

She remembered perceiving his image as the Tarot Ace of Swords and felt pity for him.

'Is that enough for a lifelong commitment, Alec? Forty or fifty years? Maybe we should just have an affair. Then if it doesn't last, we can go our separate ways and forget about it.'

He saw through her flippancy to the defensiveness of a person who like himself had been badly hurt in the past.

'No, you are too precious for that. For me, it has to be all or nothing.'

She smiled at him, placed her teacup on the tray and stood to go, needing to escape his intensity.

'Thank you, Alec, for honouring me so. You may know, but I don't yet. So please give me some time to answer.'

He stood up too and looked deeply into her green eyes.

'You can have all the time in the world, if one day you will answer yes. I will phone you when I get back next week. Let me give you a lift home.'

'No, I would prefer to walk. I have some thinking to do.'

He nodded and went to fetch her coat, fearing his haste had lost him the prize.

1 : 7

Liz arrived back home to find her flat mate Fran in a less than charitable mood.

'So where have you been for three days?' she demanded. 'Didn't you even look at the messages I took for you?'

Liz picked up the slips of paper and leafed through them. Nothing appeared urgent. She flopped onto the sofa.

'Sorry, Fran. But I've been having an amazing time with Alec. I'm around for the rest of the week now, though.'

'So he is letting you have a little bit of your own life back at last!'

'He's away on business for a few days.'

Fran regarded her more closely.

'There's something more, isn't there,' she said.

Liz nodded. 'He's asked me to marry him.'

'And you said?'

'I asked for time to think about it.'

'You what? You're not actually thinking of hitching up with that overloaded ponce? If you do, mark my words, you'll regret it.'

Fran flounced out of the lounge. A few moments later she left the flat, slamming the door behind her.

Liz sighed and picked up the phone to call Bethany.

'At last! Where have you come back from?' Bethany demanded as soon as she spoke.

'Don't you start too. I've already had Fran giving me a flea in the ear. Can I come around tomorrow morning? There's something I'd like to talk over with you.'

'Great! You can help me decorate the lounge. I'll see you at ten.'

Liz turned up at Bethany's plush commonside flat in Westfield House on time next morning to find her friend sitting in the lounge eating a late breakfast. While Liz had dressed in old clothes and covered her hair with a scarf ready to start work, Bethany was still wearing her favourite terracotta-coloured trouser suit.

'I thought you wanted to decorate, Beth.'

'I am. I've got the paint. Orange like I'm wearing and sunshine yellow to go with the suite.'

But you haven't cleared the room yet! Have you got dust sheets to protect everything? Paint trays and rollers? Brushes? Turps?'

'Oh, bugger!' she swore and sat dispiritedly on an ottoman.

'You've not thought things out very well, have you.'

'Don't you start! It was bad enough Uncle Phil going on at us all, about gatecrashing you and Alec. He said Mike and I live like we're playing a game, which we aren't bothered if we win or lose. Mike got angry and walked out.'

'Is that why Mike's not here this morning?'

'No. He's uptown, working. Dealing.'

'Drugs, cards, or stuff fallen off the back of a lorry?'

'He didn't say. But it won't be drugs. He's not that sort.'

'He's not any sort.'

Liz switched on the kettle in the kitchen and opened the serving hatch to continue their conversation.

'Was Uncle Phil right?'

'I'll have a coffee,' Bethany said, evading the question.

'Was he right?'

'Yes,' she admitted grudgingly.

'And what did he say that made Mike walk out?'

'He told Mike to stop playing everyone off against each other like chessmen. I said he wasn't, but Uncle Phil said I was the piece he played the most. I told him it wasn't true: Mike and I love each other. As soon as my parents come around to the idea, we'll get married.'

'Is that likely? I remember your Dad saying he didn't pay for your education so you'd become a gigolo's dishwasher. You could run off to Gretna Green. Or get pregnant.'

'You must be joking!'

Liz emerged from the kitchen with two mugs of coffee. She handed Bethany one and sat near her on the sofa.

'I've a bit of a problem about marriage myself,' she said.

'No! What's happened?'

'Alec Graham proposed to me.'

'Where's the problem in that? Why aren't you out buying the trousseau right now?'

'It's not that easy. I don't know if I love him. It was different when I was with Guy. I'd have accepted him like a shot. But he's not the type to get married.'

'So? Cut your losses, have your cake and eat it. Marry Alec, have an affair with Guy, and forget you ever had to live in a crummy flat-share on the wrong side of town.'

Liz shook her head.

'I don't want to live a lie the rest of my life. What if I find he has some silly habit that drives me up the wall, like playing a tune on his teeth with a biro the way Murray Scott did?'

'Not Murray Scott. When did you go out with him?'

'Soon after we left school, just before I met Jimmy Caldbeck.'

'Oh, the cad who filled you with drink and tried to turn you into a sex worker? You weren't alone – he tried it on me too. At least I can thank Dad for putting a permanent stop to his nasty little games.'

'Aye. Maybe I'm scared this is going to go wrong too.'

'Why? Do you think being in love is a weakness? It can be if you fall for men like Jimmy Caldbeck. But Alec will be worried it's a weakness too, and he's got more cause to worry about being used than you.'

'But you just told me to use him!'

Bethany put down her mug and turned squarely around to face her friend.

'Yes, I did, because like Uncle Phil said, I tend to play life, not live it, so that's what I would do. But you care far more about other people, so you're looking at it from every angle, and taking it all far too far. I think that if you care enough about Alec to ask yourself all these questions, you care enough not to have a guilty conscience when you sign the register and become Mrs Graham.'

Liz still looked unconvinced.

'But I want to be sure it's right.'

'Liz, you'll never be completely sure it's right. Tell him yes, get engaged, and keep putting off the date until you're okay about it. Don't let caution delay you too long, in case you actually do love him only to find the offer isn't open anymore.'

1 : 8

Alec played an impatient tune on the Lincoln's horn and stared at the house where Liz lived, fearing she would not come out. He cursed himself for arriving early and played another tune on the horn. The front door opened. A flurry of flower-printed cotton and cream cheesecloth hurried down the path and Liz was there beside him, her green eyes sparkling and her perfume filling the air with the scent of roses.

'I was worried I would have to eat lunch alone,' he said, feeling her exuberance lighten his own heart.

'I couldn't have let that happen after you cut your trip so short,' she replied, forgetting herself as she stared into his hopeful eyes.

An insistent hooter returned their thoughts to more mundane matters.

'I think we should drive off, Alec: there's a queue of cars held up behind us.'

He came back to the present, put the car in gear and drove on along the street.

'The business in Lebanon took no time to deal with, much to my surprise,' he said. 'Mother of course expected me to fly back home via Corinth for Easter, but I told her I had several important engagements including some lectures which I must still prepare, and an appointment with a certain friend. She said it must be a very attractive young female friend for me to stay in cold London instead of sunny Corinth for the holiday, and she is coming to stay

47

with me instead so that she can meet you. She is looking forward to it.'

'Oh dear,' Liz said, having visions of a prim, stern battle-axe giving her the critical once-over.

'Don't worry. Goldie is one of a kind,' he reassured with a fond smile. 'She'll love you.'

He paused to negotiate the car through a busy junction and turned up towards the common.

'What have you been up to while I was away?'

'Helping Bethany decorate her flat, and giving her a shoulder to cry on because she hasn't seen Mike since last Saturday. And getting the third degree from Mum after I casually mentioned you had invited me out. Dad meanwhile made fewer offensive comments about fortune telling and instead made several archaeological pronouncements which were totally wrong.'

Alec laughed with Liz and felt himself relaxing for the first time since he had left to fly abroad.

They had lunch at the Commonside Restaurant, sitting at an outside table in the unusually warm spring sunshine, so that they could look out over the common as they ate. They chatted as if they had never been apart, enjoying each other's company and the good food.

'And so, of course, I never learnt the poor fellow's name!' Alec finished, laughing at his own anecdote.

As a waiter served them coffee at the end of the meal, he paused and the laughter fell away from his face. He stared intently into her green eyes.

'Liz, I had intended to let you tell me when you felt sure of your answer. But I must know now. I cannot wait.'

Liz reached across the table and took his long, strong fingers in her slender hands.

'Alec, I knew the answer I would give before I received your telegram. Yes, I do want to marry you. I do need you, and I've missed you so much while you were away.'

At once his whole demeanour changed. He pulled her to her feet and spun her around in joy. Then he kissed her firmly on the lips. She responded more passionately, clinging to him with an ardour that surprised herself as well as him.

'Tomorrow we will go and buy to you the best ring in town. We'll visit jewellers and dressmakers and shoe shops, and you shall be dressed as the princess of women should be,' he said happily. 'And your parents can come to Briarbank, say on Good Friday, to meet Goldie and me. And you must inspect Briarbank and tell me what you want to change. Then there is the day to arrange and your dress to order, and the invitations, and the reception...'

'Stop, stop!' Liz cried, laughing in bewilderment.

'Why should I? The world is ours and we can take it!'

His impetuous desire for all to be done at once intoxicated her, and infused the week leading up to Easter. The days fled before them as they took by storm the London he knew, while she chose to ignore the London she knew which hid beneath its glossy mask. She hardly seemed to take a breath before it was Good Friday, the day she and her parents were to meet his mother.

A taxi dropped Liz at Briarbank shortly before her parents were due to arrive for dinner. She looked elegant in a purple silk Sabatina shift dress, revealed as she shrugged off her midi-length suede trench coat for Theo to take.

'Liz, at last!' Alec said, leaving the lounge. 'I was very concerned. You must meet Mother right away.'

She followed him into the lounge, struggling to replace her worried frown with a pleasant smile.

'Goldie,' he introduced: 'This is Elizabeth Kirkland, the young woman I was telling you about. Liz, meet my mother, Mrs Goldie King.'

Goldie rose majestically from the sofa, her heavily made-up face beaming amiably. Her voluminous dimensions were held in check by a wide cream skirt and a kingfisher blue blouse, over which she had slung several loops of pearls. Her fine white hair was highlighted with a purple rinse that had taken very well.

'Liz,' she said, her strong accent lengthening her name so that it sounded like Leesse. 'I am so happy to meet you. And I am sad that your delay prevents us from meeting at the airport.'

Liz stared at her, bewildered, for she was nothing like the mother she had imagined standing behind Alec. Their eyes met, and both sensed a natural affinity. Their faces relaxed, their smiles became genuine. Goldie ushered Liz to sit beside her on the sofa.

'I'm so sorry I couldn't go to Heathrow with Alec to meet you. My friend Bethany had a problem which she tried to sort out with a decanter of brandy. I will need to check on her again later.'

'Then you have every right to miss our little date, and Alec, you have no right to be angry with Liz.'

'I was not angry with Liz, Goldie,' Alec protested, pouring out some drinks. 'I simply dislike waiting alone in airports.'

'That is what he says,' Goldie said slyly, and then laughed. 'Excuse me, Liz, for I mean no harm. It is just my little bit of fun, teasing Alec. He is so humourless.'

'Oh, I wouldn't say that, Mrs King. Alec and I...'

'Uhuh, my child! To you I am not Mrs King, I am Goldie. I do not call you Miss Kirkland, do I? Though perhaps Alec does.'

'Goldie, will you please?' Alec began, handing her a drink. He winked at Liz as he gave her a soda and lime.

'Goldie will I please what? Sing one of the old songs? Take the curtain call? Or play Rule Britannia on the bow and saw?'

'You must be out of practice now,' Alec said, sitting in the armchair near Liz.

'To play Rule Britannia? Send Sam to fetch me his saw.'

The bell rang, interrupting them. Liz hurried out into the hall as Theo opened the front door. Her parents entered: short slim Nora Kirkland, looking youthful with her chestnut pageboy hairstyle; and Richard, thickset and greying at the temples, wearing a conventional grey suit and a Rotary tie held in a monogrammed tie clip.

Liz introduced them to Alec who showed them into the lounge and introduced them to Goldie. Goldie then commandeered the conversation for the next twenty minutes to ensure the ice was truly broken before the meal. She continued over dinner, asking questions to encourage Richard and Nora to talk about themselves. They did not know how to take her banter but presumed her to be a harmless and friendly eccentric. All five sat talking at the table long after it had been cleared. When Alec finally suggested they return to the lounge, only Liz and her parents arrived there.

'This certainly is a mark up on your bedsitter, Liz,' Richard said, gazing round at all the cream and maroon brocade in the spacious room.

'Alec is very nice,' Nora commented. 'Fancy his being a client of yours. At least some good has come out of your time away. You've been quite a dark horse about it all.'

'We only met three weeks ago. Time's just flown.'

Goldie entered, looking purposefully at Liz. Alec followed her in and crossed to the cocktail cabinet to pour more drinks.

'Liz, it is quite late, and you say you need to phone about Bethany,' Goldie prompted. 'I take you to the study.'

Liz thanked her for the reminder and followed her out of the lounge, too preoccupied to realise Goldie was stage-managing her. She phoned Ainhurst and chatted with Bethany's mother about her drunk friend. At the end of the call she replaced the receiver and stared thoughtfully at the numbered dial.

'Bethany means a lot to you, yes?' Goldie asked sympathetically.

Liz started in surprise to find her still there in the study. Goldie closed the book in her lap and settled back in her armchair by the window. Liz sat on the edge of the broad highly polished oak desk to face her.

'Aye, Beth does. We went to school together. She's been a good friend to me. She gives me that little push I sometimes need to get things done. People think everything comes easily to her, but that's not really the case, though she seems more strong-willed and self-assured.'

'Where you are more caring, yes? What makes you care for Alec more than anyone else?'

'I don't fully understand it, but somehow when I'm with him, everything is magic. And I can't understand what he sees in me. But he makes me feel so special. And he treats me with such reserve.'

'His restraint concerns you?'

'It makes me want to draw him out of himself. It shows me he respects me as well as loves me. I have never felt that before.'

'Alec is a strange one. He has great depths which no-one else is allowed to see. He says so little – I cannot picture you from his description. I tell Alec what I think of you: my first impressions are confirmed again and again, consciously and unconsciously. You are so different to the woman I expect him to choose. It is good that he ventures from his own circles, and fortunate that his venture brings him straight to you. As long as he obeys the will of his dear father, God rest his soul, I am proud to accept you into our family as my daughter.'

Liz blushed, speechless.

'Why are you embarrassed? It is true, is it not? Now, as I speak your eyes frown. Is there something that puzzles you?'

'Aye. Why do you and Alec have different surnames? I would have asked him later but…'

'Then it is good that I get you to ask me, for Alec is shy about his past. His father was killed by…'

The study door opened and Alec entered. Goldie nodded to him in approval. He ushered her and Liz through to the lounge. Richard and Nora stood up to join them.

Alec produced a small jewellery box from his pocket and took Liz's left hand. He gently slid a diamond ring along her ring finger.

'It is official. Now we are engaged,' he said.

'Alec, this is the happiest day of my life,' she whispered.

They clasped hands and kissed the fist they had made together, while their parents applauded in approval.

1 : 9

To celebrate their engagement, Alec threw a large party at Briarbank three weeks later. The house was filled with guests, and champagne and fruit punch flowed freely. Alec proudly showed Liz off to all his friends, delighted that she was wearing dramatic black velvet to set off his engagement present of diamonds. As his discovery and creation, she looked even more than usually special that night. Her own guests, including her parents, feared they would not get to speak to her at all for his monopolising her. Only when Sam took him aside to ask a question about the catering did Guy manage to corner her.

'Here's to the stunning *femme fatale* from the flashy jet-setter!' Guy toasted her and spun round to show off his fashionable air-force blue suit.

Liz laughed politely with a new social polish which Guy saw with concern. He tried to point out her uncharacteristic falseness in his own inimitable way.

'After seeing this party crowd I don't envy you, Lizzie babe. I sport my whistle for but a day. If you go through this hitch and hatch with that walking weasel you'll be acting for the rest of your life, and you're far too much of a new woman to kneel at hubby's feet and serve the vicar tea for long.'

'You're not jealous, are you, Guy?' she returned light-heartedly with melodramatic gestures appropriate in a silent film: 'Aye, I do believe you are, but. It's too late now - I am promised to another!'

He laughed and returned in similar style, 'Oh no! My heart is shattered, Lizzie babe. See, it lies in a puddle on the floor, over there in the corner. What a mess!'

Her laughter caught Alec's attention. Their eyes met across the room. She smiled at her fiancé and turned back to Guy without noticing Alec's frown. Alec gave Theo a casual instruction as he passed by with a tray of drinks. Theo crossed the crowded room to stand near the window and Liz, ostensibly serving champagne. Guy exchanged his empty glass for a fresh one and turned back to listen to her.

'I could never compete with your press, Guy,' Liz was saying: 'Even Fran comes a poor second. and she helps you out every spare moment she's got.'

'You're right, Liz. I almost loved you once, till I realised you're too into your signs and portents to play honorary reporter cum typesetter for me. I hope you weren't too upset by Fran's big scene, were you? When she walked out on you for "selling out to that overloaded queen"? She was only being jealous again; and it's funny how it didn't upset her that much until the flat above the Print Workshop was finished.'

'No, Guy, it didn't surprise me. I knew she had been waiting for the chance to be closer to you the moment you moved out of Uncle Harry's. So watch how many night shifts you put in at the press now!'

'Darling!' Bethany declared heartily, making Liz jump. 'So sorry I'm late - had a prior engagement. Lovely party. Glad to see it's all going so smoothly. Is that champagne? Don't mind if I do. Hello, Guy - hardly recognised you in a suit. What's the latest snippet of underground gossip to be crushed by your new *Iron Fist*?'

Guy exchanged a meaningful look with Liz, both identifying from the choking fumes of alcohol on Bethany's breath that her prior engagement had been with a bottle of brandy. Guy tried to ease the situation with a teasing grin.

'My latest is that a certain Guy Simms, editor of the infamous *Iron Fist*, is madly in love with the blue-eyed copper-haired beauty about town Bethany Broome.'

'Darling! And I thought you only had eyes for proofs!' She laughed raucously and then dropped her voice to whisper fierily in Liz's ear, 'I really do suggest you go and mingle a bit, sweetie-pie. Your dearest dear has been shooting you the most horribly jealous looks, and Guy has rather hogged you since I got here.'

Liz thanked her for the warning and tacked off through the crowd looking for a safer friend to talk to while Bethany flirted with Guy. She narrowly avoided Theo as he went to refill his tray and instead collided with her chapel priest, Father Jeremy Kingston. Father Jay was an unconventional Christian minister with a practical theology bordering on pluralism because of his work with both spiritual and physical salvation. Liz linked her right arm through his left and apologised. He tossed back his long dark grey hair and patted her hand, his thin, lined face breaking into a Mephistophelean grin.

'Do you like the fancy dress, Lisbeth?' he asked, referring to his white dog collar: 'I thought it would be appropriate for the occasion, seeing how you'll be wanting me to marry you both.'

'Enchanting, Father Jay, but does it convince people?' she replied with a fond smile.

'Not really. I did have a go at converting those archaeologist colleagues of your husband to be, but with little success yet. I'm pleased you've finally claimed your own man after all.'

'Aye, I've given up the bad boys for good. Sadly, our engagement's brought the reaction I feared in some quarters. Some of my friends think I've sold out.'

'Can they be such good friends then, to let their envy come between you? Mind, Lisbeth, the chapel will be expecting a far larger contribution from you now.'

Liz laughed at his light-hearted reference to a less than Christian criticism she had once made, knowing it was a fair comment.

Someone called for the guests to clear a space in the centre of the lounge and Goldie stepped forward. She had dressed for the party in an aggressive kingfisher blue gown with her trademark yard of pearls wound round her aging neck. Her heavily made-up face was lit by a kindly smile.

'Ah, Mrs King, a delightful lady,' Father Jay commented: 'Very proud of her career as an actress, I found, but a while since she lived up to her pet name.'

'Aye, she acted for all of five year, till she met her Arthur whom one should never mention. I couldn't wish for a lovelier prospective mother-in-law, for all her eccentricity,' Liz returned.

Goldie called for silence and asked Alec and Liz to join her in the cleared circle. They stepped forward to polite applause, Liz blushing and looking to Alec for strength. He was masking his jealousy behind a social smile which she saw through to the turbulence beneath. She responded with a glittering, provocative smile to reassure him.

She found his possessiveness an obstacle as she tried to adjust her way of life to his. His physical restraint since that heady moment when he had spun her round and kissed her with such joy at her acceptance, confused her. She could not understand why he had not responded to her subsequent advances with more than a hesitant kiss and a casual embrace. She did not doubt his affection because he showed it in every material way available but was troubled by the emotional barriers which stopped him sharing his deeper feelings with her.

'Alec, Liz,' Goldie ordered, catching hold of their hands. She turned them both around to face the crowd.

'Engagement is a time when lovers confess their love to the world,' she announced. 'Dear Alec, dear Liz, I know I speak for everyone here when I wish you both every happiness and fortune for the future. I also wish to say how happy I am to welcome Liz as my new daughter in our small far-flung but happy family. A toast to Alec and Liz.'

The guests raised their glasses and repeated her enthusiastic toast. Liz shyly buried her face in Alec's shoulder, unused to such family ceremony. He coaxed her to look up again and then delivered a short speech in polite reply. She assumed a regal smile as she listened to him speaking on her behalf as well as his for the first time; but it was a false smile, applauded by her family but despised by her friends. Bethany resolved to speak to her about it immediately after the speeches but was thwarted when Goldie took Liz to one side.

'Are you all right, my precious? Is this party too much for you?' Goldie asked her.

'I'm fine, really: just not used to this sort of thing,' Liz replied. 'Did you have a good flight over from Corinth this morning? I didn't have a chance to ask you before.'

'No, Liz. I never have good flights from Greece. Always the airline complains about my baggage and I complain about the food. Ah, Philip, there you are. Come and meet Liz.'

She beckoned over a boyish-faced young man of about Liz's age, taller than Alec and slimly distinctive in a dark green suit complimented with mint green. His collar-length hair was naturally blond and straight with a low fringe which enhanced his long ever-smiling face.

'Without Alec about? What would he say?' he asked roguishly.

'I would say, Liz, meet Philip King, my brother from Corinth,' Alec returned from behind, swift to involve himself in the introduction because of what he had so far left unsaid. Liz's quizzical frown did not surprise him, though it did Goldie. Philip naturally played up to them.

'Pleased to meet you at last, Liz, after all those near misses,' he declared without accent: 'You have seen me before, perhaps, and are wondering where?'

Liz hastily apologised for her nonplussed expression and explained, 'Alec has told me quite a bit about you, but with your different surnames I never dreamed you're brothers.'

She turned away to place her empty tumbler on Sam's tray as he went past, and turned back in time to catch Goldie glaring at

57

Alec as Philip gave a delayed, slightly cynical laugh. Goldie was whispering, 'Alec, you do not tell her,' but stopped short when she realised Liz was watching.

'I will, Goldie, but we have had so much to talk about, that was left,' he answered, and embarked on trying to talk his way out of the situation to Goldie who always saw through his explanations.

While Alec was distracted, Philip stepped forward and drew Liz aside. Philip had heard Goldie's effusive description of Liz after their first meeting three weeks before and had read Alec's letters about her, but wanted to discover for himself whether she was as wonderful as they had described her.

'Yes, I am Alec's infamous brother,' he said, keeping faith with Alec's secret: 'You would never hear the full truth about me - he disapproves of my lifestyle. And you are his intended! The man who decried all fortune tellers as charlatans and mountebanks, landed by one of the very breed he most despises!'

'I don't know: I think he despises middle-class communists more,' Liz joked warily, sensing Philip's rudeness had a more obscure motive than mistrust.

'You know what I mean,' he returned, amused by her response. 'How did you meet?'

'His chauffeur picked up my business card after he overheard me telling the owner of a bookshop about a drug dealer who was being chased up the road by Bethany there.'

She nodded towards her friend, who smiled back at them and took the opportunity to latch onto her again. Liz introduced them. Philip made a brief flippant comment about Bethany's pursuit of Pierre Eve to deter the attractive drunk and turned his attention back to Liz.

'It was all very sudden, very unlike Alec. Did you cast a spell on him when he phoned, Liz? Or did you call round and slip him a love potion?'

Bethany took instant offence at what she took to be an ill-mannered slight and belligerently demanded, 'What, d'you think

58

Liz isn't good enough for him?'

'No, Bethany,' Philip said, giving her a winsome smile to pacify her, knowing he would be foolish to argue with alcohol. 'From what I hear and see, Liz is too good for Alec - such beauty shouldn't be wasted on a man whose first love is old fossils.'

'It isn't!' Liz protested: 'Alec's got nothing to do with palaeontology - he does wonderful research into the symbolism of ancient civilisations. I knew of his reputation in the field long before I met him, and I've referred to his papers on Minoan symbolism several times in the course of my own work.'

'You have?' Bethany asked her in astonishment, drawing a slightly indignant affirmative from her in reply.

Philip laughed at them both and continued to challenge Liz.

'Yes, inheritance aside, I would have said Alec was the last person to marry. He's always been content with his housekeeper and his manservants - the thought of little children playing near his specimen cases would send him into a cold sweat. Or do children constitute another area you haven't got around to talking about yet?'

'Philip, please stop abusing your privileged position as Alec's brother,' Liz cautioned with a look of tired patience; determined not to let his impertinence unsettle her. 'Yes, Alec and I have discussed such matters, but I'm certainly not going to share our private decisions with you or anyone else. So if you'll excuse me, I'll go find something useful to do while you find a more agreeable manner.'

'Yes, Liz: could you show me to a phone?' Bethany quickly asked: 'It's about Mike.'

Grateful for her request, Liz led Bethany away from Philip and the party noise to the relative quiet of Alec's study, their departure followed by Philip's hearty laughter. Liz shut the door and crossed to the desk to offer Bethany the phone receiver as she pressed a button to obtain an outside line. Bethany replaced the receiver in its cradle.

'Thanks Liz, but the phone call was just a ruse to get you away from that Philip chappy. Though it's true I haven't heard from Mike for weeks now, which is why I sampled some of Daddy's brandy. What sort of madhouse are you getting into here?'

'What do you mean, madhouse?' Liz asked with an affected little laugh.

'So you think it's a rum set up too. You may be changing, Liz, but you can't lie to me. What is Alec doing to you? I know we're meant to be blossoming into maturity now; but I preferred you when your hair was long and natural and you dressed like a gypsy: at least the part you acted then was you. This *Vogue* cover model image doesn't suit you at all.'

Liz felt for her lonely friend whose criticism of others was born of the hurt she felt inside herself.

'We are all a thousand women in one, Bethany: this is just another facet - the same Liz is still here underneath the makeup. Try not to be so upset about Mike: he's always come back before.'

'Upset? That's about the understatement of the year.' Bethany turned away until she had controlled her threatening tears. 'He's not coming back this time, Liz. I know; and so do you - you wrote about it in my horoscope.'

'Don't believe that, Bethany. I made a mistake. Let me check it for you....'

'But you don't make mistakes, Liz. You always tell it straight from the shoulder, and you're always right. That's why you were getting more business, and why many people are sad you're giving it up now you're going with Alec.'

'And I will miss it, but you can understand Alec's point of view.'

Liz gestured to the displays of ancient artefacts. Bethany followed her hand and glanced dizzily around the room.

'I'm sorry, Liz. I know I told you to marry Alec and have an affair with Guy, but that's because it never mattered before whether I won or lost, until I lost Mike. You live by different rules, and when you followed my advice I think you made a mistake.'

'I'm not just following your advice, Bethany, and I don't think I'm making any mistake. Yes, I'm changing, but it's because I want to change, because I love Alec so. He's brought out new things in me I never knew were there. Suddenly everything has become exciting and worthwhile and new. I never expected to feel that way again. That's how I know I'm in love.'

'Then I'm thrilled for you! And I shall change the subject. Do you know a girl called Teresa or Terry Carter?'

'Not that I recall. Why, should I?'

'Not necessarily, though she seems to know about you. She came into the Antiquarian Bookshop about a fortnight ago to order a special book, limited edition stuff. Something about the Cabala, whatever that is.'

'Esoteric Hebrew mysticism. It includes things like word and number games, significant word or letter sequences in books like the New Testament, much beloved by the Gnostics. St John used it to describe Nero in Revelation with that bit about the number of the Beast being 666.'

'Is that what it is! Why couldn't Uncle Harry describe it that simply? Anyhow, while he was processing the order, the woman struck up a conversation with me about your business card despite me quietly doing my nut about the accounts. She asked me if you were the Liz Kirkland who wrote that article for the Print Workshop publication. So Uncle Harry looked at her over the top of his glasses like he does and said, "You mean my son really does have a reader? I'm surprised a person who reads books about the Cabala would read *The Iron Fist* too." So she explained the book was a present, and we got chatting about the Print Workshop. Visit over. But when she called back to collect the book yesterday, she quizzed me about you again, and she asked me to arrange for you and her to meet.'

'What does she look like?'

'Unmistakable: really beautiful but for the pan makeup she

61

uses; just the right height but for her high heels and the way she wears her blonde hair up in a bun; and a deep husky voice that would keep her in boyfriends the rest of her life. All in all, the sort of woman we'd want to scratch her eyes out.'

'Had she been expecting me there?'

'I think so, though she never let on. It was the way she looked round, as if there might be another little office. As if I would be doing the accounts at the counter if there was!'

Liz nodded thoughtfully and felt a nagging uncertainty rise inside again despite her attempts to suppress it. Archaeologist and businessman though Alec was, those roles could not account for some of the phone calls and messages he had sent and received during their last three weeks together. She opened her bag and took out the monochrome picture postcard of Beirut.

'Okay, Bethany, I'll trade you a mystery. What about this?'

Bethany inspected the picture and read the message on the reverse side: *The two-way transmitter is dead. J. K.* She shrugged her shoulders and handed the postcard back to Liz for her explanation.

'The postmark is the Lebanon, the day after that drug pusher Pierre Eve quit here and turned up dead outside Paris. The day after the card arrived, Alec flew off to the Lebanon too, saying something about *our mutual friend,* but I know for certain it's not Father Jay even though those are his initials. I keep asking Alec what it all means, because I know it could all be perfectly innocent. But each time he quickly changes the subject which makes it all seem even more odd...'

She broke off, longing to tell her friend about the unanswered mysteries she was finding in Alec's life, but reluctant to break the promise she had made to him not to discuss their relationship with others.

'It should be so simple: I love Alec and he loves me,' she cried: 'But the world around him is getting so complicated; and this not knowing makes me feel I'm drowning in his mistrust. He must have been hurt very deeply once, not to let me come any closer than arm's length.'

'I'm not surprised, when your ex Guy is chatting you up in a corner at your engagement party and no sign of his latest anywhere in sight!' Bethany scolded, but saw Liz's dismay and relented, giving her a spontaneous hug to reassure her. 'Don't worry, Liz. He'll get over it, just like you'll get over looking like a mannequin. You come over to my place and meet this Carter woman to find out what she's really about. That might make things clearer for you. And don't forget you've always got an ally in Alec's housekeeper. Even his henchmen should be good for some information.'

'Sam and Theo? It would be easier to pull a tooth than extract...'

A sharp knock on the study door interrupted Liz. She sighed with a wry smile and put the postcard back in her handbag.

'Talk of the devil, Bethany! Time to go back to the party.'

Bethany saw the new false smile return to her friend's face as she opened the door. Outside, Theo offered her a fresh glass of fruit punch. Liz accepted it and walked regally back into her new life after a few moments off. Bethany followed on, pitying her.

1 : 10

Ten days later Liz took a break from arranging her wedding to meet Teresa Carter one evening at Bethany's apartment. Though Liz arrived on time Terry had got there before her and stood at the balcony window to watch her walk down the back lane and enter the building. Liz was wearing sweatshirt and loons, with her hair caught up in a scarf and no makeup at all, her new off duty look. Bethany opened the door to her, chatting enthusiastically about their trip to the dressmaker's shop earlier that day.

Terry turned back from the balcony window when Liz entered the yellow and terracotta lounge and greeted her with a warm smile. She sported a smart navy business suit and looked as beautiful, and as heavily made up as Bethany had described. Her pensive grey eyes suggested hidden depths where emotional danger lurked.

'I am so pleased to meet you at last, Liz,' she said in a deep sensual voice.

Liz perceived her to be a hazardous lure, like a temptation to drink the forbidden Waters of Lethe before her time had come, and hastily shuttered her mind to her strangely attractive charms. As they shook hands Liz deliberately blocked the flow of her own spiritual power to prevent this disturbing woman stealing her positive force.

'It's always interesting to meet a fan, Terry, especially a woman who I hear reads both the Cabala and *The Iron Fist.*'

'Yes - I have a sort of unholy interest in the black arts. Bethany told me you're a professional fortune teller. She says your Tarot readings are very accurate. Do you practise any other methods of divination?'

'Aye, I'm a qualified astrologer and an amateur graphologist.' Despite her apparent openness, Liz was wary, aware that Terry was not telling the whole truth.

'Amateur? Come on, Liz! What about solving dreams, getting premonitions and reading palms?' Bethany said. She finished uncorking the bottle of wine Terry had brought for the occasion, upturned two glasses and a tumbler, and continued, 'Wine, Terry? I won't ask you Liz, 'cause I know the answer.'

'Why, don't you drink wine?' Terry asked Liz, sounding surprised.

'No, nor any other alcoholic drink,' Liz replied, wondering why she should ask that when most people would take Bethany's comment to mean she was a heavy drinker. She tried to take over control of the conversation.

'Would you like me to do you a Tarot reading, Terry? Quite confidential, and no charge.'

A strange expression passed across her face, and briefly Liz saw her psychic image as a cracked rock, a shattered altar of stone stained with unacceptable sacrifice.

'I'd rather not. Though fortune telling fascinates me, I wouldn't mix with it,' Terry politely refused, a statement so at odds with her psychic image that Liz knew it was a lie. Before she could comment Terry asked, 'What made you get involved in fortune telling originally?'

Liz gave a bitter little laugh and said, 'I didn't choose to get involved: it sought me out. For more than half my life I ran away from it, just as you appear to be doing, but I only found contentment when I turned to face it and learned to accept it all: my premonitions and all the rest.'

Terry gave her a penetrating look, her grey eyes burning into Liz's green eyes. Liz felt a surge of emotion behind Terry's thoughtful expression, suggestions of pleasure and control which warned her she was being manipulated.

'Have you ever joined any fortune telling circle or association?' Terry asked.

'No. Whenever I found one and checked it out, I was always struck by the way they all descend to the level of the lowest common denominator. It has never tempted me to seek further.'

'Then how did you come to face up to the challenge of your gift?'

The telephone rang, interrupting them. Bethany answered the call and offered Liz the receiver, teasing, 'Old flame for you, Lizzie babe.'

'Guy? What does he want?' Liz asked, taking the receiver from her.

'A favour,' Guy replied: 'On Dad's advice I'm bringing out a cover mag for *The Iron Fist* as it's getting a bit too subversive in parts - you know how it is. The new mag's called *Helicon*, the name of a magic mountain, and it's aimed at the older teenage type, full of articles on teenage issues. The first edition will go to press in a month and it'll be published while you're away on your honeymoon. Trouble is, personnel: most of the Workshop crew are busy with *The Iron Fist*, and Fran's still got her studies. We've got around it a bit, but I wondered if you could fill a page a month and also make up the horoscopes - we're calling that *Astro Mountain*, and it'll be another full-page feature...'

'Hold on, Guy,' Liz interrupted: 'Hasn't the teenage mag market already reached saturation point?'

'In some fields, true; but this is a completely new approach - hip arts and gothic. Glossy pages, colour pix, ads in the back, and articles like you've never seen before, written for the youth of today by the youth of today in the language of the youth of today. Get the picture?'

'Sure, G. S. But isn't it a bit gimmicky? Especially if it's only monthly: little continuity.'

'We've sussed that one out with market research. You'll be part of the linkup. You can write about any basic theme you like as long as you can keep it up for at least nine issues. Fran suggested *Viewpoint*, a commentary on teenage issues; or a *Life in London Diary*. I'm afraid it would have to be for love until we're established.'

'That's okay. I'll have a go at *Viewpoint*: should be able to keep that up for at least three years. When do you want my first attempts?'

'Two months' supply ASAP if you can. We're doing a stock in hand like the other mags: standard articles in two to three months before press day. Interested in a problem page?'

'Only if you're positive there's no-one else to do it; and on one condition, that my identity isn't disclosed: Alec wouldn't like it.'

'Sure, Liz: I'd do that anyway with you doing three features. Thanks: knew I could depend on you. Maybe Fran won't be so bolshie about you and Alec now. Incidentally, there's been some mouth-shooting about you and him underground: a defunct mag making a last gasp for air with libellous conjecture. I scared off the smut seekers as best I could, but a couple of reporters still want to stick their necks out, mainly as some guy with a Jon tag's been checking out an Elizabeth Graham for the last two months with no success. Any gen?'

'No, Guy; but thanks for the support, and the warning. D'you have anything more on the Jon fellow?'

'Not much. He must be a bastard 'cause everybody's shit scared of grassing on him when I asked for more. Tell you what, come over to my office the day after tomorrow, p.m. and I'll show you the lay-out and give you the lowdown.'

'Okay, Guy: I'll see you Wednesday at three at the press.'

Liz replaced the receiver wondering how she had let herself in without protest to write three free articles a month. She found her one-sided part of the conversation had Bethany light-heartedly speculating along different lines.

'"Alec wouldn't like it"? That's a new one from you, Liz. Since when have you been responsible to anyone but yourself?' she teased.

'Since I got engaged,' Liz answered. She returned to her seat and asked, 'Where were we?'

'Bethany was just staying you went to school together near here,' Terry said.

'Was I? Must have had another black-out,' Bethany remarked with a frown of disbelief, raising her empty wineglass. She got up to refill her glass and top up Terry's.

'Liz, would you mind having your photo taken with me?' Terry asked, pulling out a disposable camera.

'I'm hardly dressed for it,' Liz protested.

'You look fine to me: just take off your scarf.'

'I'll get my camera too,' Bethany chipped in: 'Have to record for posterity the last time the world will ever see Liz with no makeup and no legs!'

She produced a Nikon camera from the wall unit and quickly set it up with a bulb switch to take a picture of the three of them.

Terry took two pictures of Bethany with Liz and then got Bethany to take four pictures of herself with her. They finished with another two group shots taken on Bethany's camera. As Bethany put her camera down by the wine bottle on the table and poured another glass, she chatted about Liz's phone call again.

'I take it Guy phoned on business: it was obvious from the smartly arranged trip to the press, the anonymous favour and writing an article. Are you two going into the blackmail business?'

Liz thought Terry's eyes had narrowed for a brief second. She ribbed Bethany in reply to see whether she could draw a more definite reaction from the visitor.

'Aye; we're going to finger Jon and you. You should give up the gripe water: it makes you do silly things; and this Jon guy's not a man to trust.'

Even Bethany saw Terry react to this and sobered up. 'You're not joking, Liz, are you,' she said.

'Fear is the key,' Liz cryptically replied, 'But *perfect love casteth out all fear.*'

She looked Terry in the eyes. Terry hastily averted her gaze, her conscience too laden for her to parry such quiet force. She got up to place her glass on the sideboard and turned back to face them both, leaning against the table with one arm behind her back.

'Will you continue telling fortunes after you get married, Liz?'

'Only in magazines from now on,' Liz replied wistfully. 'But what I will get instead is the best library in existence on symbolism in ancient cultures, and all the time in the world to indulge in it.'

Terry glanced at her watch and reached for her handbag.

'I'm sorry, girls. I have to go earlier than I had intended. I've just remembered I've got a report to complete for tomorrow.'

'Why, what do you do?' Liz asked.

'Nothing special: I'm a secretary uptown for my sins. It's a good job - just the commuting from Croydon gets me down at times.' She slipped on her coat. 'Hope to see you again, Liz. I'll give you a ring later in the week, Bethany.'

And with that she left. Her abrupt departure left Bethany very curious as they had originally planned to make an evening of the meeting.

'Why the change in you both, Liz? Do you think she has something to do with the Jon chappy too?'

'Maybe, and from what Guy said on the phone, that might not be such a good thing. That's why I'm going to see him the day after tomorrow, not just for the new magazine.'

'Then I'm coming with you. It'll give me something to do and your Alec less to worry about. Will you want to meet Terry again if I can arrange it?'

'That depends on what Guy has to say. Have you seen my head-scarf?'

1 : 11

Bethany arrived at Briarbank in her maroon Volvo 246 in good time to drive Liz to the Print Workshop for the meeting that Wednesday, only for Alec to hold them back. He had just taken delivery of a garden sculpture by Bethany's father and wanted Liz to be the first person to see it in pride of place at the centre of the back garden lawns. Liz dutifully humoured him, though she was not as taken with Stanley Broome sculptures as he was through knowing more about their background. She and Bethany made the sort of comments he expected when the statue of two female-torsoed sea monsters was unveiled, and then escaped.

Bethany raced Liz over to the Print Workshop, only to find soon after they arrived, that she should not have worried about being late. They dashed through the reception area to avoid a stormy scene from Fran and entered the unusually silent press floor. There Guy was helping another of the co-operative workers finish the paper feed adjustments needed to begin a big print run. Guy stepped aside and waved to them in greeting before turning back to his work.

As they waited Bethany remarked, 'By the way, Liz, you remember those photos we took the other night with Terry Carter? When I collected the film today after processing none of them had come out. The shop said the light had got in, like the back of the camera had been opened.'

'How odd,' Liz replied. 'That means I don't have anything to show Alec. Did my scarf turn up?'

'Funny you should ask: no, it didn't. Sure you don't want to meet her again?'

Guy gave the order for the press to start rolling and joined Liz and Bethany by the door.

'Sorry you had to wait so long. Didn't realise it would take all that time - we were worried the paper had got damp. Come through to my lair.'

They stepped back out into the passage as the machinery roared into life. Guy led the way to his office, continuing to talk about his beloved press as he strode out ahead of Liz and Bethany.

'Completely *passé* now, of course, with your modern electronic technology, but you sure can buy a cheap working press these days, and find plenty of technical expertise to help run it for peanuts too. But don't you be telling your Alec that, Lizzie babe, or he'll be making another killing.'

'What makes you say that?' Liz demanded sharply. She got no reply.

Guy showed them into a dusty lino-floored room with grimy windows and tired old metal business furniture, all of which made the office look as though it had not been cleaned properly for a decade. He moved some drawings onto the floor from his large black-topped bottle-green desk and spread out some paste-up sheets in their place for Liz and Bethany to inspect opposite him.

The sheets were the preliminary mock-ups for *Helicon*, visual demonstrations of the style Guy was aiming for with the magazine. He spent half an hour explaining details about the new co-operative project, and his enthusiasm was so catching that even Bethany willingly offered to try her hand at the *Life in London Diary* feature, with a promise of no tears if he thought her attempts unfit for publication. Liz felt more confident too that the magazine would have a chance in a competitive market.

'But of course I shall not tell Alec that, to stop him making another killing,' she promised wryly. 'After all, has he already been warned about one?'

She threw down the monochrome postcard of Beirut on top of the paste-up in front of Guy. He frowned at her and picked it up.

'Do you really want me to have this, Liz?' he cautioned. 'And in what capacity are you showing it to me? A reporter or a friend?'

'A friend, I suspect,' Bethany answered, recognising the card. 'Who did you say was asking for an Elizabeth Graham?'

Guy turned the postcard over and saw the initials J. K. at the end of the message informing Alec the two-way transmitter was dead.

'A man called Jon,' he admitted. 'But this is pure coincidence.'

'The timing suggests not,' Liz disagreed. 'The card was posted the day after Pierre Eve died near Paris, after he had fled from Briarbank because Alec and I had confronted him about his drug racket. The day after the card arrived, Alec left for the Lebanon too.'

Guy nodded thoughtfully, still tempted to think Liz was being over-imaginative despite the timing.

'What do you want me to do about it?' he asked.

'I don't really know, Guy. I have no qualms about the part Alec played in it, but I would like to know more about these possible adversaries of his, if only to pray for them.'

Guy almost choked at her words. Even Bethany smiled.

'Lizzie babe, that J. K. is probably a gun runner to have been in the Middle East at that time; and the reputation of this Jon boy is not the sort to become a goodie two shoes on the strength of one *Ave Maria* either.'

'All the more reason to pray for them, Guy.'

'Then ask Alec: I'm not going to risk my butt over them.'

His uncharacteristic alarm surprised Liz: Guy was usually too much the champion to fear. She tried to shock him out of it by standing up as if to leave, her expression remote, her hand outstretched for the return of the card.

'My apologies, Guy. I shall not bother you again with my requests.'

He saw three free articles a month about to disappear through the door and changed stance at once.

'You know I don't mean it like that, Liz. I'll find out what I can for you, sure I will. But we're just a little concern here: either of those men could wipe us off the map with a snap of their fingers. I have to be careful. That's why I suggest you ask Alec first – he has enough clout to be able to return as good as he gets.'

'I don't think Alec is prepared as yet to confide in Liz to that extent,' Bethany commented.

'And that does not bother you?' Guy asked Liz in dismay.

'That is my concern,' she sharply replied.

His face fell. He was alarmed to discover the markedly different persona Liz had already taken on for Alec, leaving behind the natural easy-going personality he had admired her for a year before. He sensed that if he did not warn her now, he would have to stand ready later, as Fran dourly warned, to pick up the pieces.

'I think you are making a mistake, Liz. I know you're not doing it for the money; but whatever your motive is, it is wrong.'

'When love is the motive, it cannot be wrong,' she snapped: 'At least, that's what you told me the day I realised you were married to that press.'

Bethany hastily stepped in to prevent a flareup of the arguments Guy and Liz had exchanged at the end of their brief affair.

'I think we should be going, Guy,' she said, standing up: 'I'm meant to be working on your father's Inland Revenue return today.'

He nodded and handed back the postcard to Liz.

'My best astrologer - my only astrologer - and I alienate her!' he said ruefully in a near apology. 'My advice about J. K. and the Jon boy is simple, Liz. Tell Alec and then stop worrying about it. I'm sure he's the type who'll see to the rest. Bury yourself in writing me the most wonderful horoscopes, and I'll make your three pseudonyms famous in every fifth house in Westfield Street.'

'All four of them? Some recommendation!' Bethany retorted.

Guy showed them out laughing, glad that Liz was friends with him again before she left to return to that veneered world he so despised, where so much more was hidden than ever came to the surface, even to psychic minds.

1 : 12

As Liz dressed on the morning of her wedding day, she found herself wondering whether she was doing the right thing in marrying Alec. Events during the previous two weeks had done little to dispel her doubts.

Directly after her meeting with Guy at the Print Workshop, she had asked Alec again about the postcard from Beirut. He had felt offended by her questioning his previous reassurances. When she told him what the Print Workshop reporter had said and described her meeting with Terry Carter, he had belittled her fears and dismissed Guy's warning about the mysterious Jon X.

'There are plenty of Elizabeth Grahams in London already without anyone looking for a new one,' he had said.

This would have satisfied her had she not overheard him later sending Sam to investigate the story. When she asked him for an explanation, he had told her not to worry and diverted her with details of their wedding arrangements.

She tried to accept his reluctance to confide in her by seeking to understand the causes, but feared his fears and insecurities would choke her love if she could not dispel them. To cope she imagined the mysteries were part of a problem-solving game he had created for her which she could work on using whatever resources she found to hand. So far, she had met with little success.

As her dressmaker fussed with the flowing skirts of her ivory crepe de Chine wedding gown, she turned to Bethany, hungry for her support.

'Am I doing the right thing, Beth?'

Bethany put her concern down to wedding day nerves and gave her a reassuring hug.

'Of course you are, Liz: you'll never keep him otherwise. I trusted Mike to do the right thing, and where is he now?'

'You doubted Alec like I doubted Mike; and now I'm not so sure that you were wrong.'

'Nonsense! You're just feeling nervous. You love him, don't you?'

'Desperately. I can hardly wait for tonight. But if he loves me as he says, why doesn't he feel the same? You know he's only kissed me once, the day we got engaged. All the rest comes from me, and I can tell he struggles with it.'

'Perhaps he's been holding back to make sure you weren't pregnant by an ex. Or maybe it just shows how much he respects you. I thought Mike loved me but he only used me. I must have gone wrong somewhere. But you've struck lucky, so take your chance while it's there.'

'Aye. I keep thinking this time I'm too lucky - I'm so scared this dream's about to shatter like all the rest.'

Alec's two limousines arrived at the Kirklands' house to take the bridal party to the chapel. The dressmaker helped Liz don her veil and then marshalled Bethany and the two six-year-old bridesmaids into the black Lincoln with Nora Kirkland's help. After they had all left the house fell silent.

Richard Kirkland sat patiently in the lounge wishing his morning suit was more comfortable and waiting for his daughter to come down the stairs, while she spent a few moments in prayer before the ceremony. When she finally appeared, she looked such a beautiful fairy-tale princess that he caught his breath. Proudly he escorted her to the waiting white Oldsmobile, the door held open for them by Theo who had dressed for the occasion in full chauffeur livery. As Theo drove them away, they followed the custom of their birth county and threw good-luck pennies out of the rear windows for the children to collect in the street.

'You're putting Cumberland well behind you now, Lisbeth,' Richard remarked, settling back in the leather seat: 'Your Alec talked of moving to Cheshire next year.'

'I'm putting a lot more than place behind me, Father,' Liz replied, gazing at the beautiful bouquet of orchids in her lap.

'I know you are,' he said, and patted her left hand. 'We've had our differences in the past, but your young man has brought out the best in you. I'm so proud of you.'

He patted her hand again. She squeezed his fingers and gave him a nervous smile.

'Thank you, Dad; for everything - even for the times when we fell out. Perhaps you were right more often than I cared to admit.'

The limousine drew up outside Father Jay's plain Victorian brick-built chapel. Alec had wanted to hold the ceremony in a grander church but Liz had refused and both her father and her priest had supported her. Now she felt reassured to be entering the familiar friendly building for such an important life event. In the porch waited Bethany and her two second cousins, dainty in pale yellow satin, ready to take her train. Liz paused on her father's arm outside the chapel for the customary photos and then went inside.

Over two hundred people had gathered for the ceremony: every pew was taken and some late attenders had to stand at the back. Heads turned to watch the bride walk down the aisle on the arm of her proud father. In one of the front pews Nora Kirkland sat smugly with Liz's brother Ricky and his wife Sophie, while on the other side Goldie clutched a handkerchief and hid the excesses of her emotional display behind a large-brimmed kingfisher blue hat.

Liz and Richard joined Alec and his brother Philip in their morning suits at the altar rail and the ceremony began. The congregation vanished from Liz's mind as she concentrated on the vows she and Alec exchanged. For her those vows were pledged for life: she hoped that Alec believed the same. They felt like strangers as they smiled at each other and exchanged rings. Then Father Jay pronounced them man and wife, and Alec kissed her again.

From that moment time flew by. First, they faced the army of photographers, both amateur and professional, grateful for a dry though overcast June day for their wedding pictures. Soon the party moved on to the formal reception at Pembroke Lodge with a five-course meal and speeches, and more photographs.

Then suddenly it was evening and they were going away together, just the two of them in Alec's Lincoln, with tin cans rattling behind and stones in the hubcaps. Alec tolerated the tricks only because they were traditional and drove around just two corners before he stopped the car to remove its adornments. To avoid his brother's practical jokes, he had kept their destination that night a secret. Instead of flying straight out to Crete as he had led Philip to believe, they stayed overnight in a London hotel before flying on to more distant Peru in the morning.

They stood together for a moment hand in hand outside the hotel's open glass doors. At last Alec was letting her hold his hand, Liz noticed. He looked at her in her moss green going-away dress with her hair loose, unexpectedly seeing again her eclipsed fortune-teller image, and realised how little he really knew about the depths of the woman he had just made his wife.

'Welcome to my world, Mrs Graham.'

'Oh, Alec; I must be in a dream.'

'It's no dream: it's an adventure - the first of a lifetime of adventures reserved solely for us.'

She was overjoyed to hear his commitment to their marriage

was as deep as hers and squeezed his hand.

'Come on then, Alec: we've got a date with an adventure, and it doesn't like to be kept waiting!'

They laughed and hurried into the bustling lobby of the hotel. Soon they were alone together in the peaceful solitude of their own suite.

It was the moment Liz had longed for in the five short months they had known each other. She had taken great care in choosing her trousseau to appeal to Alec despite his puritanical taste. While he phoned room service to book a morning alarm call, she disappeared into the bedroom to change. She shut the curtains on the close June dusk and dimmed the lights to a flattering level for intimacy. Then she arranged herself provocatively in her black satin and lace and called out for Alec to join her.

He had not realised what she had been doing and stood in the doorway, taken aback to see yet another facet of his wife that made her a stranger to him. Dismayed by his reaction, she rushed across to reassure him and cradled his head in her hands as she kissed him with the full force of her desire. She gently divested him of his jacket and waistcoat, and slid her hands beneath his shirt to caress his chest. Her closeness and her hunger for him melted the rigid straight-jacket of his self-control. His reserve shattered.

He threw her onto the bed in his desire for possession, tearing off her clothes and forcing himself upon her too soon. Her desire for him enabled her to accommodate his selfish love making and respond to him. But afterwards she lay back in the pillows, disappointed that his continuing insecurity and rigid self-control were still marring their relationship. She prayed that in the days to come she would be able to reassure him enough for him to drop his guard with her, so that they could make love with more tenderness than his first-night lust to claim his right of possession.

Chapter 2

Card 11: The Enchantress

Interpretation: a powerful woman

feminine or subconscious power

After their return from their honeymoon, Alec and Liz held an informal Saturday evening theatre party for a few guests. Shortly before their guests were due to arrive, Liz was sitting at her dressing table with a copy of *Helicon* on her lap, her mind far away as she waited for Alec to finish dressing. She had long since finished her own preparations and looked dramatic in a bronze Sabatina creation which draped all the material of the bodice and the skirt elegantly together in a large circle-clasped belt. Her heart-shaped face was perfectly framed by her well-coiffured black shoulder-length hair.

Alec wandered back into their bedroom as though he had lost something. Half-dressed in a light blue shirt and the waistcoat and trousers of his slate grey suit, he carried a blue tie in one hand and a grey one in the other to ask his wife to choose which one he should wear. She came out of her reverie and vacantly looked up.

'Oh, the tie. I got you a new one, dear, to match that suit. It's on the bed.'

He thanked her and exchanged the two old favourites for the new tie while she smiled into the pages of her magazine. Her husband liked to comment on the vanity of women without recognising that same vanity in himself. He saw her smile and sidled over as he knotted his tie to see what she was reading which amused her so. She teasingly covered the name at the top of the page, forcing him to ask her about it.

'This is the first edition of Guy and Fran's latest venture, *Helicon.*'

'Ah, the subversives' answer to copy convention. And you are ever the astrologer, I see; at the horoscopes page: twenty phrases in a hat.'

'Nonsense! A true astrologer studies the planetary

influences for the month and relates them to each sign in turn.'

He laughed fondly to see how easily she gave herself away but continued to play her game by hiding the fact that he knew her secret. He recognised the usefulness of the game in making her content not to stray into those areas of his life which for her safety he dared not let her enter.

'Is that the astrologer's picture in the corner? Elliot Mayfield - what a name! Is he accurate?'

'Listen. "Pisces: Mars is chilling out in your anti, Virgo, and causing a load of hassle between you and your dig mates, so now it's time to decide which lover is number one. But don't be blue: August is gonna be ace, with wicked news at work that really brings in the bread at last. You Fish People are a lot better at the top of the tree than the Establishment realises, and you're a helluva lot tougher than Big Daddy thinks. No-one'll walk over you if you get your deals done on the new moon, round the 17th. So keep smiling: ambition-wise you'll really make the scene."'

'Far out!' Alec mocked, waving his hands in the air. 'I hope you will not have to choose between lovers this month, Liz, or expect to get wicked news at work. And on the 17th I'll lock you up.'

She gave him a sweeter than real smile and replied, 'Thank you dear. Did you realise I'm a lot tougher than you think?'

'From your tone I have to say, no I did not; though I can assure you I am not a big daddy yet. But who am I to criticise the learned Elliot Mayfield?'

'You aren't so modest when you criticise our elected Prime Minister, dear.'

The telephone interrupted them. Alec hurried across to the bedside cabinet to pick up the receiver before the housekeeper answered the call downstairs. A look of concern passed briefly across his face as he was connected with Athens airport.

'Goldie, at last! What's happened?... Of course I was worried. You promised to phone from Heathrow at four and it's now nearly seven. Is it serious?... Yes, I appreciate it's serious for the people involved. What I meant was, is Athens airport closed until further notice?... Fair enough. I'll apologise to Andrew and arrange for you two to get together next week... Isn't tomorrow a little soon - you might still be waiting in Athens... Oh, she's rung off.'

He threw the telephone receiver back in its cradle, exasperated by Goldie's unpredictability. Why did she never humour him the way his wife did?

'You don't need to be psychic to guess that was Mother, Liz: not lost in a shopping spree along Oxford Street after all, but delayed at Athens airport until tomorrow because of some political trouble there. Terrorists or something; but she's quite safe, though for all she said I'm still not clear about the details.'

'How disappointing for her: she was so looking forward to meeting Mr Ferry at the theatre tonight. Did she work with him once?'

'In the year dot. If you want to know more ask her when she finally turns up. It's a very over the top story from the episode about her years of fame.'

The telephone buzzed with the housekeeper's warning that the first of their guests was about to arrive. Alec slipped on his jacket and offered Liz his left arm to escort her downstairs. She linked her arm through his and gave him a quick kiss on the cheek, her lips leaving a bow of scarlet lipstick above his beard. Laughing, she wiped the lipstick off with a paper handkerchief. He shot her a spoilt scowl for the delay. She scolded him with an indulgent tut and propelled him out into the hall before he could make the delay a significant one.

Their theatre party comprised six including themselves. Their guests were Sean Cookson, the playwright of *Sunset*, the production they were going to see; Fran who had patched up her quarrel with Liz and had been asked by Guy to review the play for *Helicon*; Harry Simms who was diplomatically standing in for his son and had ensured that Guy was too busy at the press to attend; and Bethany whose father knew Sean Cookson and had asked Alec to create a believable introduction between the playwright and his daughter, hoping she would forget Mike for a new love with Sean and leave her father's brandy decanter alone. Goldie and Andrew Ferry were to have made the supper party eight had Goldie been able to persuade the modest actor away from the theatre after the performance.

Fran was the most disappointed to learn they would not be dining with Andrew and Goldie that night. As the guests mingled in the Grahams' lounge, Bethany was trying Alec's vodka bottle for a change, while Sean was trying not to drink so much that he made a fool of himself and took up with Fran instead, judging her to be a much more useful, natural and younger companion for the evening and a far less dangerous one. Harry and Alec soon locked into a deep conversation about old books and symbolism. Liz coaxed lonely Bethany out into the garden to get her away from the vodka and Sam's over-efficient service. The two friends drifted across the lawn to the focal point of the stone sea-monsters sculpture.

'Marvellous, isn't he!' Bethany spat bitterly: 'Such great insight, such gifted artistry! You know that statue's a product of a warped mind. Mummy got a broken arm for that one!'

Liz nodded. The twelve years since Bethany's father had started physically abusing his wife and daughter, had passed far more quickly and somehow turned out far better for her than for the friend she had once envied for having everything.

'Remember that time you got even with him, Beth, when you painted clothes on that nude study?'

Bethany smiled with wry embarrassment. 'Could I ever forget that? It was gloss paint too! That's how I met Mike: literally ran into his car. He must have been in a fix like that himself once - as soon as he saw Daddy chasing after me, no more questions: just "jump in" and away we drove...' She shook her head reflectively at the sculpture. 'You know, I could swear Daddy had something to do with Mike's leaving. God knows he tried often enough.'

Liz followed her words back into the past and recalled a frozen moment of Alec talking on the study telephone while she had been slipping on her coat in the hall. The colour drained from her face as she realised what had happened. Alec had offered Stanley Broome his help in persuading Mike to leave Bethany in return for that sculpture; and his method of persuasion had not been financial but physical: he had threatened Mike with Sam and Theo. Suddenly her game of finding out what Alec did not want her to know, was no longer fun.

'Let's go back inside,' she suggested quietly.

'Yes, of course: you look worse than I feel,' Bethany agreed in concern.

In the lounge Alec was organising the seating arrangements for the party to travel in in his two cars over to the theatre. He firmly insisted that Fran should join Liz and himself in his black Lincoln driven by Theo, so that Bethany and Sean could get to know each other better with Harry as chaperone in the white Oldsmobile being driven by Sam. The two groups agreed to meet up in the theatre foyer on arrival, and set off in the late afternoon sunshine of a hot August day.

2 : 2

The Lincoln arrived at the theatre first. While Alec went to check their box reservation, Liz and Fran bought programmes for their party and waited for the others in the foyer, chatting about the production's garish publicity poster.

'It's certainly eye-catching,' Fran remarked.

'But the colours aren't at all sympathetic,' Liz objected.

'That's because it's functional - you can't miss it.'

Liz suddenly paled and stumbled back, clutching Fran's arm to steady herself. Fran felt her clammy touch and hastily looked round for a seat, fearing she was about to faint. Finding everything suitable already occupied by others, she hurried her outside into the fresh air. They almost collided with Bethany as she arrived with Sean and Harry.

'What's up, Liz?' Fran asked her once they were outside. She got no response.

Bethany recognised her pale face and vacant look and replied, 'It's one of her premonitions, Fran. There's a seat over by the bus stop - I'll take her there. Tell Alec not to worry: she'll be right as rain in a couple of minutes.'

Before Fran could object Bethany guided Liz to the bench by the bus stop, which stood on the corner between the High Street and the theatre's access lane.

'You could choose a more opportune time, Liz: that storyteller was just getting interesting,' she joked, trying to jolly Liz out of her vacant stare. She held her hands and wondered how they could be so cold on such a hot August evening.

Liz gazed at the cars driving past them on the High Street. She felt detached from the world about her, elegantly out of place against the grubby suburban backdrop. When she said after a delay, 'That isn't the problem,' even her voice seemed curiously distant.

'What was the last thing you saw beforehand?'

Liz pointed vaguely to a copy of the garish publicity poster on the bus shelter. Bethany scanned the poster and shook her head.

'No, there's no clue there, unless something goes wrong with Shifty Sean's play tonight.'

'That's too remote,' Liz said remotely: 'I usually get feelings about things I'm affected by, like the time that landlord tried to evict some of us from that house.'

Her thoughts wandered back through the events of the last two hours, with the gathering of the theatre party and the journey there. As her senses began to clear, she noticed a powder blue Jaguar with the distinctive number plate PS 1 move across the unfocussed surroundings.

The car turned off the High Street onto the theatre access lane and drew up at the stage door. Before it had stopped, the nearside front passenger door swung open. The stage door also opened and a slim casually dressed man with cropped hair and a weaselly shaped face shot out. He dived onto the front seat and had barely closed the passenger door after himself before the Jaguar sped away again.

'Two of them?' Liz remarked, puzzled.

Bethany looked at her in concern, having seen three men in the car. Liz realised from her expression how she was sounding and tried to bring herself back to the present.

'I'll be fine now, I promise. Let's get back to the others.'

Bethany reluctantly walked with her back into the crowded theatre foyer. In the lee of a pillar, Harry was giving Alec a kindly lecture about keeping a better eye on his wife's well-being. Alec broke away as soon as he saw Liz and hurried to her side, his assessing eyes narrowed in concern.

'Liz, how are you now? What's wrong?' he demanded.

Fran stepped back out of his way, bridling at his arrogant manner. Bethany had drunk enough of his vodka to counter whatever Alec might throw at her and prepared to face up to him. Their fears proved unwarranted. Liz easily melted Alec with a calm smile and an assurance that she was fine. She linked her arm through his and led him across the foyer towards Harry and Fran.

'Alec, is there a reason why the registration number PS 1 should be significant?' she enquired.

'Psi?' he asked in concern, repeating the number as the Greek letter. 'Where did you see that?'

'It drove past us while we were outside,' Bethany said. 'It stopped to pick up someone from the stage door. The driver was a bit odd, like something out of a horror film, with little piggy eyes.'

Alec considered her report and shook his head. 'No, must

be a coincidence. You've been letting your feelings get the better of you, Liz.'

Sean re-emerged from the crowd, his self-important manner announcing he had succeeded in using his influence to achieve an advantage.

'Yes, Alec, if you and Liz want to deliver your apology to Andrew before the performance starts, the ASM will take you backstage now.'

Alec thanked him and took Liz's arm. They followed the young female assistant stage manager into the wood and canvass world backstage, leaving Sean to take the rest of the party to their box for the performance. The ASM led the Grahams down a poorly lit brick passage linking the principals' dressing rooms, to a battered door with Ferry's name stencilled on a piece of card dropped in a loose metal holder. As she knocked briskly the five-minute bell rang.

'Dr Graham and company to see you, Andrew.'

'Thanks, Jeannie,' the actor called back, and opened the door to them. He was an elderly man with a fit upright bearing. His lined face was exaggerated by make-up to look mortally tired, but when he saw Alec the effect was broken by a broad grin. He jovially slapped his biceps.

'Alec, me old boy! How are ye?' he greeted, his accent a pot-pourri of all the parts he had played in his long and varied career.

A wry smile tarnished Alec's usual reserve. 'As fit as I can wish, Andrew. Alas, I'm the harbinger of bad news: Goldie has been held up in Greece by some terrorist trouble at Athens airport. She's quite safe, but she has been delayed. She asked me to give you her apologies for tonight. She'd like you to come over and see her tomorrow afternoon instead.'

'Aye, of course, laddie. But don't be standing on the doorstep. Come in and tell me who's yer little lady friend.'

He stepped aside to let them enter his untidy dressing room.

'This is the little woman,' Alec replied, waving towards

Liz.

'And she is too!' Ferry exclaimed, chuckling at their private joke. Years before Alec had confided that he would only wed a pocket-sized princess because of his own relatively short stature. Even wearing heels, Liz was two inches shorter than him.

Ferry sat down on a chair with his back to his make-up mirror. Liz looked around for a place to sit too but found every surface covered with the paraphernalia of his trade. She remained standing beside Alec near the door.

'So you've finally got hooked, Alec! And I can see from your blushes, milady, that you've no' been a missus for long,' the actor teased.

'Just since June,' Alec answered for her. 'And how are things with you, Andrew?'

'Amazin'. I've no' had such luck in a long time, thank the Lord.'

He paused to drink from a pewter tankard engraved with the logo of Neptune's trident in a decorated circular border. His serious manner suggested to Liz that his luck had brought him rescue from failure rather than success.

'Lucky in what way?' she asked.

The old actor turned to look her squarely in the face.

'Another Goldie, I see,' he commented to Alec, and then replied, 'Lucky to be here. I'm like a cat wi' nine lives. Last Monday the safety curtain just missed falling on me. Saturday night, was it, some lunatic drunk driver almost ran me down outside my flat. And no' long back I near got trapped in a fire. God keeps smiling on me though.'

Alec frowned. After what Liz and Bethany had told him only a few minutes before he knew Andrew had far more cause for concern than he appeared to realise.

'It sounds as if someone is after you, Andrew. You should go to the police.'

'Polis? Och, no: they were only accidents. And who should be after me? I'm no' but a rundown actor playing the principal part in a second-rate play.'

'How about the Angus twins?' Alec warned, not diverted by Andrew's expressed humility.

The actor's face fell.

'How d'ye ken them?'

'Liz and her friend Bethany saw their blue Jaguar about a quarter of an hour ago, picking someone up at the stage door. Is Sandy Angus up to his tricks again?'

Both Liz and Andrew looked sharply at Alec; her expression dismayed to discover her husband's lie; the actor's painted face further contorted by a worried frown.

'So ye ken that, Alec. But ye dinna ken it all.' His manner sharpened. 'Well, that's the polis had their chance. Alec, now you think on. There's been rumours in the club about a certain lady who's greatly interested a friend of yours. I couldn't get hold o' ye then, so around the middle o' June I tipped off someone who could do summat about it. But now't's happened since, except to me.'

The two-minute bell rang outside. Andrew turned to his mirror and busied himself with a powder puff to declare the conversation closed. Alec ignored his hint.

'What young lady?'

For a split second Andrew's eyes glanced through the mirror at Liz. She knew instantly he meant her. Guy's warning from before the wedding came back to her, about a man called Jon who had been looking for an Elizabeth Graham. Were the two connected, and were they were the cause of her premonition, she wondered, but dared not voice her concern while the actor and Alec were taking such care to exclude her from their conversation.

'It's too long to explain now, Alec: I'm about to go on. If you come for me in good time tomorrow afternoon, I'll tell you everything then. There, that's them calling the beginners on stage. I must go.'

He stood up and shook their hands, thanking them for

coming to see him and wishing them an enjoyable evening.

'I'll be there at two thirty tomorrow,' Alec promised him. 'Break a leg.'

Andrew laughed and bustled off down the passage towards the stage. As he receded into the gloom Liz saw the ghostly cowl of death envelop him. She paled again and clutched Alec's arm.

'What do you think of Andrew?' he asked, unaware.

Her chill voice replied, 'That actor is a great man; but a hounded one. And a dead one.'

2 : 3

Early next morning Alec strolled into the kitchen, dressed formally in his favourite blue summer suit and carrying Liz's dressing gown. She was sitting at the kitchen table with a pot of coffee, her thoughts distracted by the recurring dream she had had in the night. In the dream she had drawn eight cards from her Tarot pack in four pairs, each pair the Minor Arcana ten of swords followed by the Major Arcana card thirteen, Death. In each pair the Reaper's sickle beheaded a different man: first Andrew Ferry, then a young man with a weasel face, the third a young man with short hair and porcine eyes, and the fourth a mature stranger with an arrogant Teutonic look. The meaning of the dream was clear: those four people were about to die, were perhaps already dead.

'You forgot your housecoat again, Liz,' Alec chided, slipping her dressing gown over her shoulders.

'I'm sorry - I didn't want to wake you. Would you like some coffee?'

He brought a mug over and sat opposite her at the table to watch her unconscious expression as she filled it.

'What's up, Liz? Guilty conscience?'

'Alec, would you send Theo over for Andrew Ferry right

away? He's in great danger.'

Her request took him aback though he was careful not to show her that. He gently covered her trembling fingers with reassuring hands.

'What sort of nonsense is this?'

'It isn't nonsense!' she insisted, grasping his hands: 'Four people are about to die, and he's one of them. The dream was quite definite - the same four over and over and over again.'

'Liz, however bad it may have seemed, it was only a dream. If it will make you feel better, of course I'll tell Theo to take you over to collect Andrew, as soon as you've got dressed and had your breakfast. It would mean you'll miss chapel, of course - I can't go because I must wait here to collect Mother.'

His drift from consoling to patronising, spurred her out of her blue mood into reactive affront.

'Yes, of course! And I can call on Bethany too on the way over, to make sure she hasn't died of alcoholic poisoning!'

He smiled fondly, relieved to see her spirit returning, and chose not to rise to her taunt.

'Yes, I noticed Bethany's tearful tête-à-tête with you in the corner last night before they all left. Harry and I were watching Sean manfully struggling to resist the temptation of too much free whiskey and Fran the sociable reporter, and Bethany failing to resist the temptation of too much free vodka while being totally oblivious to the temptation of one social-climbing Irish playwright. Surely she didn't feel for that cad that much?'

'Mike? Yes, she did. And I was very disappointed to realise the part you played in his disappearance.'

'What part was that?'

She glanced through the window at the Stanley Broome sculpture at the centre of the back-garden lawns. The telephone stopped her from saying more. As Alec stood to answer the call on the wall phone, she slid her arms into the sleeves of her dressing gown and busied herself preparing breakfast.

'Good morning, Philip,' Alec impatiently greeted the caller.

'How are things in Athens now...? Oh. Has Goldie managed to get away, then...? Yes, I've got that - Gatwick at ten past ten - we'll be there to collect her. I'll call you at the villa in four hours to confirm she's taken over Briarbank once more... Yes, it is as bad as that...! You too, Philip. Goodbye.'

He replaced the receiver and turned to inform Liz he would be leaving in half an hour to collect his mother from Gatwick. His manner made her feel more like a secretary than the little woman.

'Yes, dear: one egg or two?' she starchily replied.

Before he could reply the telephone rang again. He answered it hastily but found the call was for Liz and handed the receiver over to her.

'Hello, Mrs Graham speaking,' she announced formally.

'Good morning: Miss Broome calling. Are you in?' Bethany returned chirpily.

Liz laughed in surprise to hear her friend's good mood, her own improving spirits pleasing Alec.

'No, Bethany, I'm not in. Have you recovered yet from last night?'

'If you're not in on that number, BT must have made some miraculous improvements. Of course I've recovered from last night. Can I pop round for a little visit? I've just realised this morning what a cranky bore I've been recently. I'd like to apologise, and to prove to you I can be happy sometimes too.'

'Then you're very welcome to come around, but I must warn you, you won't be my only visitor. I'll pick you up on my way over to collect our other guest, if that's all right: in about half an hour.'

'Fine. Who is it - anyone I know?'

Liz hesitated before she replied, 'I'll let you find that out when we get there.'

Bethany heard the uncertainty in her voice and sensed Liz needed her cheerfulness that morning, just as she had needed Liz so often in the fortnight since her friend had got back from her honeymoon.

'Okay, hurry round as soon as you can. I'll be waiting for you,' she said and closed the call.

Liz went upstairs to dress and re-joined Alec some ten minutes later, cool in a pale green cotton sundress for the radiant August day. As she entered the kitchen, the telephone rang again. Alec answered the call. The caller introduced himself as Detective Inspector Marner.

'Yes, I am Dr Graham... Yes: Andrew Ferry is a friend of the family... Why? What's happened to him...? Oh! I'll come over at once. Are you at liberty to tell me how and when?... No, it was only to tell my mother why he won't be able to see her this afternoon... Sadly no: she should be landing at Gatwick in a couple of hours - delayed by that hijacking in Greece... No, I would rather my wife collected her to break the news - Mrs King can be somewhat emotional at times... I'll see you shortly, then, Inspector Marner, in about half an hour.'

Alec replaced the receiver and turned back to Liz, his expression grave. 'I owe you an apology.'

'How did Andrew Ferry die?' she asked, dry mouthed.

'Apparently a heart attack last night, which doesn't explain why a detective inspector is investigating. So you will watch what you say about Andrew from now on. I do not want you involved in this at all if possible - people would misinterpret your clairvoyance.'

'Don't you worry, Alec!' she retorted, indignant that he had ordered rather than asked her. 'I shall be the dutiful wife and go collect your mother for you and tell her the bad news for you, and I will phone Philip for you at lunchtime....'

'No: that's business. Must you take Bethany with you?'

Liz noticed his subtle side-step from a direct instruction to an imperative request, but would not give him that concession because she intended playing Bethany off against Goldie to make the meeting easier for herself.

'I can hardly back out now. Anyhow, Goldie likes Bethany.

She won't mind her being there.'

'Then you had better run along, to give yourself enough time to pick Bethany up before going to meet Mother's plane!'

Liz stood up with a curt 'of course', upset by her husband's imperious manner. Alec knew from her reaction that she would wilfully ignore his hint about Bethany. While she was upstairs retrieving her handbag before leaving with Theo in the Oldsmobile, he went to the study to make a quick phone call. Liz arrived at the Westfield House apartment block fifteen minutes later to find no Bethany at home, just a scrawled note saying she had been called away unexpectedly about something to do with Mike. Liz travelled on to Gatwick deep in thought, suspicious of her husband and not looking forward to the meeting that lay ahead.

2 : 4

Liz arrived at Gatwick airport at precisely the time Alec had stipulated, to find the charter flight Goldie had managed to acquire a seat on, had been delayed a further twenty minutes. The crowded airport was stifling that sultry summer morning. With time to spare, Liz sought refuge in the small chapel to pray for the souls of Andrew Ferry and the three other men in her dream. A few minutes later she emerged to hear a distant tannoy message calling her to the airport information desk in the International Arrivals Hall. She hurried back down to the ground floor and introduced herself at the desk. A uniformed woman promptly handed her a telephone receiver.

'Liz? Alec here, still with Detective Inspector Marner. He wants to see you about Ferry too, right away.' His curt tone warned her he was not at all pleased with the turn of events.

'Then you'll have to give my apologies to him, Alec, for right away is impossible. The arrivals board says Goldie's plane has only just landed. She'll be at least twenty minutes clearing customs. Then I have to take her to Briarbank; and you wouldn't want me to leave her alone there after breaking the bad news.'

He appreciated the excuses she was giving him for her non-involvement, useless though they were in the circumstances.

'What about Bethany?' he asked.

'You know very well about Bethany: by the time I got there she'd vanished!'

'Good: one less to deal with. After you've collected Goldie, get Theo to bring you both over to the police station. I'll take Goldie home with me in the Lincoln while you see Inspector Marner, and you can follow on with Theo afterwards.'

Liz agreed reluctantly and fondly bade him goodbye, wishing he could be with her through the difficult morning ahead.

As she returned the receiver to the uniformed woman at the desk, a hand tapped her right shoulder. She swung edgily round to find a smart, attractive young woman beside her who she remembered all too well.

'Terry Carter!' she greeted in dismay.

Terry had dressed for the day in a pale lilac summer suit and heels, with her blond hair pinned up on her head. Her over-effusive joy at their meeting almost cracked her pan make-up.

'You remember me!' she gushed in her distinctively deep and husky voice. 'What a surprise seeing you here! I'd just come to meet some people for work when I heard your name on the tannoy. Thought it couldn't possibly be you as there must be lots of Elizabeth Grahams around, but I had a look anyway, and here you are! And so stunning! Marriage really suits you. Come and meet my colleagues. They've an interest in your line of business too.'

Terry took Liz across to two businessmen standing in a space between the crowds near the arrivals board. She introduced them as Hendrik Gerber from Utrecht, a tall, lean man with a long, rugged face and a bushy greying-blond beard; and Rolf Krueger from Mannheim, a broad-faced Teuton with narrow intense eyes and a firm handshake. Liz recognised Krueger at once and caught her breath: his head was the fourth and last she had seen severed by the Reaper in her recurring dream that morning. She used courtesy to conceal her dismay and waited for an opening in the conversation to warn the stranger.

'We are honoured to meet so famous a lady, Mrs Graham,' Hendrik Gerber complimented with an air of omniscience, taken by her air of vulnerable beauty.

'Indeed, I had intended to try to see you while I am in London: so much has been said about your occult skills,' Rolf Krueger added, perceiving the young woman to be a malleable weakling he could easily dominate.

Liz was astonished to hear two business people crediting her with such a good reputation for her poorly rewarded years of dedicated but unsung work as a psychic, and went on guard at once.

'I haven't practised for over three months, and I'd have said my reputation before then was rather infamous,' she joked woodenly.

'Your fame has clearly spread further than you realise, Liz,' Terry said.

'I know how far my fame has spread, Miss Carter.'

Their eyes met. Her statement echoed hollowly in the secretary's ears, for even her continued presence there with them proved it to be a bluff. By leaving her uninformed, Dr Graham was endangering his wife and helping towards his adversaries' ends; and Liz seemed so fragile and helpless that Terry felt tempted to take her hand and lead her away before their world destroyed her. But Terry also enjoyed being a party to conflict and resisted the temptation. She broke their challenging stare by sweeping her blonde fringe across her forehead with her left hand.

'What brings you to Gatwick, Liz?'

'Collecting my mother-in-law. She should have arrived

yesterday, but that trouble at Athens airport delayed her.'

On the arrivals board the information beside the flight from Athens changed to *In Customs Hall.*

'Yes, our Greek delegate should be on the same flight.' Terry added to her colleagues, 'Phineas left in good time to make sure he doesn't miss the AGM this year.'

Gerber make a comment in Dutch which drew a contemptuous laugh from Krueger. Liz regarded the German more closely, sensing from his faintly malevolent air that his early demise might not be so surprising.

'Hendrik says Phineas will have had his just desserts flying charter class for once,' Krueger translated for Liz, unsure of the reason for her attention.

'What are you delegates for?' she asked him.

'The conference we are here to attend,' Gerber replied with a hint of a smile.

'Is that the Athens flight leaving the customs hall?' Terry asked to deflect them.

She hurried off across the concourse to the rails protecting the walkway from the customs hall as another group of travellers emerged through the automatic smoked-glass doors with laden luggage trolleys. Gerber apologised to Liz and turned to follow her. Before Krueger could go after them, Liz caught his forearm to hold him back.

'You are living beneath the Sword of Damocles, Mr Krueger,' she warned. 'I implore you to change your ways - if you stay as you are you do so at your own peril.'

His naturally arrogant expression was eclipsed for a moment by a startled look. Without further comment he impatiently shook off her hand and strode away after Gerber. Liz turned away to find her driver Theo standing beside her. She sensed his mistrust behind his impassive minder's face.

'I had to warn the man, Theo: he'll be dead before the end of the month.'

'And 'e 'as no intentions of being late for that meeting,'

Theo cryptically observed.

The automatic doors slid open again and Goldie sailed forth from customs, resplendent in a salmon pink trouser suit, effortlessly propelling a loaded baggage trolley. Her silver hair had gained an unusual purple and yellow tint which bordered on the comic, but Liz did not notice that because of the news she had to break to her. Theo flagged her down and directed her towards Liz as he took the trolley from her. She sailed on over and greeted Liz with a maternal embrace, her silver bangles jangling on her arms. Liz's wooden response confirmed at once what she suspected, that something was amiss.

'Tell me, little Liz, why does Alec not come to meet me too?' she asked. 'For twenty years I catch planes to see Alec and Alec brings cars to meet me. But today he sends you. What is wrong?'

Liz turned to face her squarely. 'Goldie, I have bad news to break to you; but for both our sakes I would prefer us to be in the car and away from all this noise and bustle before I start.'

'Is Alec seriously ill?' Goldie demanded, fearing that she had misinterpreted the signs.

'No, Alec is quite well. But something bad has happened and we are both somehow involved. So I would rather not say anything more until we're alone.'

Goldie reassuringly patted the hand that restrained her but understood Liz's caution. She sensed that someone was watching them both and looked up sharply to catch the eye of a young blonde who was standing with two psychically untrustworthy men. With them was the strange Greek representative who had sat beside her during the cramped flight. With such psychic eddies moving about them she kept her curiosity under control until she was sitting beside Liz in the Oldsmobile and Theo was driving them through the Surrey countryside towards London.

Liz broached the subject before she needed to prompt her.

'Alec was about to leave to collect you this morning when

we got a call from the police asking him to go straight over to see them.'

'What do the police see him for?' Goldie asked, bracing herself for the reply.

'Andrew Ferry's death.'

Goldie turned away, dumfounded; for once at a complete loss for words despite all the warnings. She expected to cry and pulled out a handkerchief, but crumpled it up between her fingers, feeling only shock. Liz awkwardly clasped her left hand.

'I'm so sorry you had to arrive to such bad news, Goldie, but Alec said it was best you should know as soon as possible. It was a shock to us all, and you knew him better than we did.'

'Yes... How...?' Goldie said vacantly.

'They said it was a heart attack, but I'm not so sure. I had a recurring dream about it this morning, and I had a premonition of trouble outside the theatre last night. And when Alec and I met Mr Ferry backstage before the performance he seemed to be worried about something. He told us how God had saved him from some nasty accidents in the last fortnight or so. Alec said they sounded like threats, not accidents, and told him to go to the police. But he said they'd already had their chance. He arranged to speak to Alec again later today. But now it's too late.'

'So you meet Andrew. Is he not such a wonderful man: so self-possessed, so calm and composed, so caring for all God's creatures...? You do not?'

Liz tactfully chose not to tell Goldie that her brief look of dismay had been caused by Goldie's grating constant use of the present tense to describe the dead man.

'When Alec asked me what I thought of Mr Ferry later, I said "A great guy, but a hounded one. And a dead one." Thirteen hours later the police phoned to say he was.'

'So you could tell... Poor troubled man. May God grant his soul to rest in peace at last, away from all the troubles of this world.'

'But Goldie, it's not just Andrew Ferry who's about to die! He's just the first, living on borrowed time with the shroud of death round his psychic body. There were three other faces in my dream too: time after time the same four. I've just met one of them, in the airport while I was waiting for you. I tried to warn him but he wouldn't listen. Why is it they never do?'

Goldie squeezed her hand, knowing well the loneliness and distress that went with the type of psychic vision Liz had.

'We can only carry the message, Liz. That is enough - we cannot do more.'

Liz nodded and looked away at the view across the silver birches of a Surrey woodland beside the motorway. She turned back to fret.

'But now the police want to question me, and they won't understand my second sight. We're going straight to the station now, so that Detective Inspector Marner can interview me while Alec takes you home.'

Goldie searched her face, concerned by her uncharacteristic fear. She saw its cause was not guilt but worry about doing something of such official importance without Alec to support her.

'Calm yourself, little Liz. God watches over you. You know how to sign the rosy cross to protect yourself from the snares of the Evil One. God always keeps you safe, my daughter.'

Liz gave her a rueful smile and relaxed a little, nodding to acknowledge she was right.

'Like you, little Liz, I see something wrong in all this. Usually I ask Alec to solve such riddles, but while Alec is good at getting answers to questions, you are good at seeing backgrounds. So Liz, you go: you find out for me, instead of Alec who is always too busy to find out the full story. Why does Andrew die? What causes his heart attack? And Theo, you will say nothing to Alec. Nor you, Liz, for he would wrap you in cotton wool and put you in his bank vault with all his precious antiques if he could. And remember, if you need help, I can still turn men to putty in my hands.'

'But where do I begin? Alec will tell me nothing,' Liz objected, not sure that this idea of Goldie's was such a good one.

'Listen to the police inspector. Then return to the theatre and Andrew's dressing room - I shall see no-one stops you from going there. Then you can go to his apartment; but perhaps they stop you from going there. And remember this: if it is foul play Andrew himself guides you, for his blood cries out from the stones on which he fell.'

2 : 5

At the police station a pleasant detective constable showed Liz into a bare, windowless office containing a battered desk which had been bolted to the floor, a phone and three hard-backed chairs. She sat down where invited and accepted his offer of a cup of tea while she waited for Inspector Marner. Alone in the grim room, she wished she had been able to speak to Alec for more than a moment at the reception desk before the constable had escorted her away, and she wondered how Alec would want her to approach the interview. The door opened again and Inspector Marner strolled in with a thin file under one arm.

'Sorry to keep you waiting, Mrs Graham,' he said pleasantly as he sat opposite her.

He was a tall, lean man with searching eyes, but his pleasant manner masked a hard, calculating core. Liz sensed he was not to be trusted even though he had done her no wrong. Her distrust conflicted with her belief that the circumstances of Andrew Ferry's untimely death required her to answer any police questions with full honesty.

'I shouldn't keep you long - I only want to confirm a couple of points. Did you meet the actor Andrew Ferry?'

'Yes, last night - my husband introduced me to him backstage just before the performance. He was playing the part of McInnes in Sean Cookson's play *Sunset*.'

Marner relaxed, anticipating far fewer problems getting the details out of her than he had with her husband. Her innocent trust gave her a vulnerable air which tempted him to pity her, but he had loyalties elsewhere and a job to do: he could not afford to let pity clash with those.

'Please go on,' he encouraged.

'We met in his dressing room, on the five-minute bell. Alec had to apologise to him because Goldie was still stuck in Greece waiting for Athens airport to be cleared, so she couldn't make the theatre supper with him last night.'

'I see. Who is Goldie? And what was her relationship with Andrew Ferry?'

'You make it all sound so sordid; but there really wasn't anything like that involved. Goldie is Alec's mother. I believe she had acted in films with Mr Ferry years ago, before she married.'

'Uhuh. And after your husband apologised to Andrew Ferry, were you able to talk to him at all?'

'Yes, we did. Mr Ferry thanked God for being lucky lately, but I could tell he didn't mean good fortune so I asked him in what way. He told me he'd almost been hit by a safety curtain, he'd almost got run over by a drunk driver, and he'd almost got trapped in a fire. He thought they were accidents. Alec didn't agree. He told him about a car I'd seen outside the theatre. Mr Ferry took a swig from a tankard as he thought about this. Then he said how he'd tipped off someone about a club because someone Alec knew was interested in some young woman, only nothing had happened since except to him. But then the two-minute bell went and he had to go. So they arranged to meet again today, and that was that.'

She remembered the actor walking away along the dim

passage with the cowl of death darkening his body and felt his shadow touch her from the other side.

'You mentioned a tankard: could you describe it for me?'

'Aye: it was pewter, a sort of presentation tankard with a fancy scroll on the handle and some engraved decorations - a circle and Neptune's trident, I think - I couldn't make out much from across the room. One thing I did know was, he wasn't drinking alcohol: I don't drink myself so I would've smelt it in the air at once.'

'So you don't think his story was drink talk. What about the car you saw outside the theatre?'

'The powder blue Jag? That was another odd thing. I'd felt a bit faint when we'd arrived at the theatre so I went outside for a breath of fresh air. While I was sitting on the bench by the bus stop, a Jag sped past us. It stopped to pick someone up from the stage door and drove on. There were two of them, though one would be bad enough: he looked a nasty piece of work. I even dreamt about him last night - more of a nightmare, really; those little piggy eyes in that macabre head beneath the sickle on card thirteen; just like Mr Ferry and the stranger with the weaselly face and the man at the airport - what was his name, Krueger? But now I'm just rambling - it's the car you want to know about, not my dreams. The registration number was PS 1, only Alec called it Psi and asked Mr Ferry if Sandy Angus was up to his tricks again. That's when Mr Ferry said about the club.'

'And Dr Graham arranged to speak to him further about it this afternoon? Well, that seems to have given me a pretty clear picture, Mrs Graham. If you think of anything else, though, do give me a ring.' Marner placed his business card on the desk for her.

'Certainly, Inspector. Before I go, there is one thing I'd like to ask you. How did Mr Ferry die? Alec said you'd told him it was a heart attack. But if it was only natural causes, why are you asking all these questions?'

'A fair question. Mr Ferry collapsed on the stairs to his flat and died in the ambulance on the way to hospital. Late last night someone phoned us from the theatre and made the same allegations you've just told me he made to you. In the circumstances we have to investigate and do a post-mortem; but it's pretty clear that Mr Ferry's death was natural and no more than an unfortunate coincidence. Andrew Ferry lived alone, and this was his first big break as an actor for many years. He can be forgiven for using his fertile imagination in his desire to create even more sensation. That same talent had helped to make him so successful in his heyday.'

Liz sensed the inspector was being informative only to mislead her from questioning Ferry's death further but chose to play along.

'How sad, Inspector. At least there'll be no scandal, no dragging up the past.'

She stood up to go, wondering whether she should ask Marner for permission to visit the actor's dressing room and apartment, and by doing so risk a refusal. If Ferry's death was due to natural causes as the Inspector had said, she rationalised, no crime had been committed, no clues had been left, and therefore no permission was required. She gave him a parting smile and left with the constable he had phoned to show her out.

Once she had gone, Marner picked up the phone again to dial out, wondering what it was she had left unsaid. As his call was answered, he saw a movement at his door and looked up.

'Ah, hello, Jon - if you would hold on for a moment. What is it now, Mrs Graham?'

'Sorry - I forgot to pick up your card?' she said sheepishly, her shoulders tense after hearing that name again.

She picked up the card from the desk and re-joined the constable in the passage outside. As she left the building, she kept telling herself the name Jon was very common. Her thoughts kept replying that the coincidences were becoming too frequent to be accidental. When she climbed back into the Oldsmobile outside, Theo saw the disquiet in her face and asked her what was wrong. She told him what Marner had told her about Ferry's death.

'So Dr Graham's not the only one to think 'e were done in. 'Ow much did you tell the D.I. in return, ma'am?'

'I told the inspector whatever he wanted to know, of course. Why d'you ask?'

'It probably don't matter to you, ma'am: you've got nothing to 'ide hanyway. But the word is steer clear, though 'e's never put a foot wrong yet. They say 'e can read your mind like a book, so you can't 'ide nothing from 'im; and 'e don't always deal straight.'

'Thanks for the tip, Theo, but I think he was dealing straight with me; except when he tried to convince me it was natural causes. Though there was that phone call to Jon after he thought I'd left... Tell me: do you help Alec out like this too, act like a sounding board for him as well?'

'Dr Graham trained me, ma'am. It's 'is orders for me to look after you, so that's what I'm trying to do. Ma'am.'

'Point taken: I won't question again.'

2 : 6

Liz entered the theatre by the stage door expecting to give a long explanation to be admitted, but the doorkeeper let her pass without comment. She walked into the deserted shadowy maze backstage, confident she knew the way to Ferry's dressing room. But the name plate on what she thought was the right door read *Jack Marshall*. Then she remembered Marshall had been Ferry's understudy: she was not in the wrong place after all. The blatant example of the show having to go on left a bad taste in her mouth. She cautiously opened the door and looked inside. The room had changed too. All was now neat and tidy: all Ferry's personal clutter had gone.

'Didn't take Jack long to move in, did it!' said a bitter voice from behind.

Liz spun round to find the assistant stage manager standing in the doorway.

'No, it didn't, Jeannie. You were fond of Mr Ferry?'

Jeannie nodded and joined her in the dressing room, shutting the door behind them.

'None of the rest of them were good enough to do up his shoe-straps! I remember him from the old days - the fifties films on Saturday night TV when I was a kid. One of the old school, he was; and there's not many of them left now. But none of these bit-part players had the humility to learn from him. They still think true greatness comes without pain.'

Jeannie's praise of Ferry and her contempt for the other actors surprised Liz, for the ASM looked to be younger than herself, brought up with television standards of instant acting, not the studied performances of the old theatres and opera halls. Then she saw the tears glistening in Jeannie's eyes as her fingers fumbled with a small black pocket diary and understood.

'You were the one who phoned the police last night, weren't you?'

Jeannie nodded. 'But they wouldn't listen to me. He had left his diary behind here. So I called round to his place on my way home to return it, 'cause I knew how much it meant to him. I got there just as the ambulance men were carrying him out. He looked awful - sunken eyes, grey face, blue lips, shallow breath. "Andrew!" I cried. He caught hold of my hand. "Pass the diary to Goldie," he said. But then he started wandering. "You must warn the little woman that I've failed," he said - he was most insistent about that. And over and over again he told me, "This is no accident, Jeannie." It was the last thing he said.'

She broke off and looked away at the makeup mirror. Only twenty-four hours before Andrew had been sitting there laughing with her about incidents from more than thirty years ago and his casual professional friendship with Goldie King, Goldie Gaston as she had been known then. Andrew had held

Goldie in great regard, though Jeannie could not understand why when she had apparently abandoned him as a friend for over ten years, only to reappear in his life when his problems had ended. And Goldie apparently had great faith in this Elizabeth Graham, from her phone call to the theatre just before the young woman had arrived. Something about Liz drew Jeannie to her, despite her model-perfect appearance. She sensed that she could safely trust her.

'Andrew used to confide in me. He had lost everything he had in life through drink: wife, family, home, money, talent, work even - everything. Then he found a new way of living, without drink; and he started to get work again, and he began to hope for a house again sometime. He didn't dare hope for a family, but I loved him. He said he was a born liar and a scoundrel, but I found he was the sort that couldn't lie. That's why it hurt so much when the police ignored him about his club. He didn't like something that was going on there: he said he didn't escape from one trap just to fall into another. But someone must have believed him 'cause he's dead now, and his heart was as strong as an ox.'

'What club was he so upset about?'

'The Psychic Society Incorporated, of course: Equity has never played those sorts of games.'

The society's name was like a revelation. One moment, Liz was wondering how all the scattered pieces of the jigsaw fitted together; the next she saw them all drop into place, so obviously that she struck her forehead with her right palm for being so slow.

'What a stupid idiot I've been! Psi, PS 1, the Greek letter ψ in the circle! Jeannie, can I look in that diary? I need the society's address.'

'Keep the diary, Mrs Graham: that's what Andrew would have wanted. You're here on Goldie's behalf to find out why he died. He even called you a second Goldie last night after you'd gone. That's why you'd cause such problems, he said.'

Liz took the diary from her and leafed through the address pages in the back. The Psychic Society was listed with an address in the London W1 district. Below that was listed the Peace and Sincerity Institute in Chelsea. Liz saw the initials and wondered whether the institute was a part of the same association. A society which played games with its name might well award its members presentation tankards for service. Liz glanced round the dressing room, wondering where that potential piece of evidence had gone.

'Jeannie, something's missing here: a pewter tankard with a design engraved on it, a bit like this.' She picked up a stick of greasepaint and drew a Greek letter psi in a circle on the mirror.

Jeannie recognised the symbol at once. 'You're quite right, Mrs Graham. I haven't seen that tankard since Jack moved in here this morning. Andrew didn't have the chance to take it home himself, but maybe someone else has for him. Come on, I'll take you over: it's only around the corner.'

They left the theatre by the stage door. Liz's white limousine and chauffeur daunted Jeannie as she sat with her in the back and directed Theo through the suburbs to a nearby residential area. The Oldsmobile drew up outside a block of flats so new that unused building materials still lay about the front lawn. Jeannie led Liz through the main door and up the stairs. She stopped a few steps below the third-floor landing.

'This is where Andrew collapsed, on his way up. Not a mark.'

'Why didn't he use the lift if he was feeling so unwell?'

'He was fighting fit! There was nothing wrong with his heart at all - he could race up these stairs, even put me to shame. He'd have thought it was indigestion.'

Liz heard Jeannie's unspoken grief in the bitterness of her outburst and tactfully led her on up the stairs to the actor's third-floor apartment. Jeannie unlocked the front door.

'He used to send me over here for things during...' Her voice trailed off as she saw the change there since the night before. 'Where's everything gone? All his things, his little bits and pieces?'

She ran inside to check that everything had not simply been tidied away. Liz followed more slowly, noticing the austerity of the threadbare carpets, the thin curtains, the tired second-hand furniture, the lack of ornament. She contrasted it with the untidy clutter of Ferry's dressing room when she had met the aging actor the evening before.

'Nothing!' Jeannie cried in anguish from the bedroom. She turned away from the empty wardrobe and dresser, and fell back onto the worn three-quarter bed to grieve at last.

Liz left her to weep, knowing her tears would bring her some relief. She tried the living room phone and heard a dialling tone. Her call to Briarbank was answered by the housekeeper, Mrs B, who told her that Alec had not yet got home with Goldie after seeing Inspector Marner. She warned her she would be late back for lunch and closed the call. Then she returned to the bedroom where Jeannie was pulling herself together.

'I'm sorry, Mrs Graham - I didn't mean you to see me like this.'

'It is no shame to mourn, Jeannie; just as it is no shame to love. Don't think that Andrew has gone - he is just in a different room now. He still sees you, and now he knows how much you love him. He will not leave you lonely in this empty room.'

She looked up at the one personal item left in the flat, an old framed cross-stitch sampler of the Serenity Prayer: *God Grant me the Serenity to accept the things I cannot change, Courage to change the things I can, and Wisdom to know the difference.* An overwhelming sense of the need for haste came over her.

'Jeannie, I have to go: something tells me I must catch them out before they have the chance to expect me. Can I give you a lift anywhere on the way?'

Jeannie shook her head. 'No, I'll be fine here. Just need a little time... Go carefully, and good luck.'

Liz nodded her thanks and left.

2 : 7

As Liz emerged from the apartment block Theo started up the limousine expecting to drive her home for lunch. Instead, she instructed him to take her to Cremorne Grove in Chelsea.

'That ain't P.S.I., is it?'

She knew from his tone that if she told him why she wanted to go there, he would not take her. His comment reassured her that her deduction was correct.

'It's just a place Mr Ferry mentioned in his diary.'

Theo reluctantly drove off towards the capital. He took her to an industrial area on the north bank of the Thames near the Chelsea flour mills. Cremorne Grove ran parallel to the river for about a mile, a concrete avenue of factory walls and wire fences. The Peace and Sincerity Institute stood halfway along, a two-storey post-war factory behind wire mesh with two ways in through the fence: the office entrance at the centre of the brick facade, and the factory gates to the loading bay on the right of the building.

Liz noted the Institute's position but let Theo drive on past two more factories before she asked him to stop. After he had drawn the Oldsmobile over to the kerb, she dropped the black diary in his lap to distract him and stepped out onto the cracked pavement.

'Look after this for me till I get back, Theo: it's Andrew Ferry's diary. And if I don't turn up in half an hour, come and fetch me. I'll be at the Peace and Sincerity Institute.'

She slammed the door and marched smartly off while he was still getting over the surprise gift of the diary. He slipped the book into his shirt pocket and leapt out to fetch her back, but hesitated when he saw how far she had already gone: his orders did not go as far as manhandling her to keep her out of trouble.

'Get back in the car, you idiot! Alec'll murder you when we

get back, if P.S.I. don't get you first!' he called out after her.

She ignored him and walked through the Institute's open gates. Her surprise at finding the factory open on a Sunday, turned to bewilderment when she found that though the entrance was unlocked, no-one was about. For several minutes she waited in the reception foyer for someone to answer the desk bell. Then curiosity got the better of her. Despite the risks she decided to explore the deserted premises.

Three pairs of double doors led from the reception foyer into the factory. The doors opposite the entrance were padlocked. The other pairs opened onto matching side passages. She cautiously advanced along the dark corridor behind the left doors first, acutely aware that she had penetrated far further than any security-conscious business should have allowed. The thought briefly crossed her mind that she might be walking into a trap, but the spontaneity of her decision to go there made her dismiss that idea. She tried some of the doors she passed to see if she could find someone at work behind one.

Most of the doors were locked. The few that were not, opened onto offices scattered with papers similar to the work-in-progress sheets Liz had seen on Guy and Fran's desks at the Print Workshop. From this she deduced the factory was a printing press too and composed an unlikely excuse for her presence there based on her articles for *Helicon*.

The last door on the ground floor passage was labelled the dark room. A large notice warned people not to enter when the red light above the door was on. The red light was off. Liz tried the handle and the door opened. An automatic low amber light switched on in the windowless room as she stepped inside. The galley-like room was furnished with laminated workbenches and fitted shelves which crowded around her. Photographic processing equipment occupied every available space: enlargers, developers, sinks, tanks and rows of chemical containers. An emergency exit door was situated below the amber light at the far end of the room. Was it an optical illusion in the dim lighting, Liz wondered, or did she really see the emergency door move slightly as she came in? She stepped over to try the bar but found the door was firmly shut.

Beside the exit stood a work-surface used for studying the results. A dozen photographs lay there together with some containers and several rolls of negatives. Above them, other lengths of negatives were pegged out to dry on a piece of string. The area looked as though the photographer had just been called away from working there. Liz picked up one of the pictures to see what the subject was. She dropped it in alarm when she saw it was herself.

With a pounding heart she looked more closely at the photo to work out where it had been taken. Her green sundress and the crowded surroundings placed the picture firmly at Gatwick that morning while she was waiting for Theo to retrieve Goldie from the crowds outside the customs hall exit. The photograph was an accurate but unflattering portrait. Her compassionate eyes appeared aloof rather than accepting; a hint of disdain pulled down the corners of her mouth, and her stance was defiant.

The photographs warned Liz that for her own safety her games with Alec had to end, for the person who took the pictures might all too easily take far more another time. Despite what her husband might say about the rashness of her visit to the institute, she had to take some of the photographs home with her to show him what she had found there. She snapped open her handbag and slid a print inside, plus three handfuls of film containers and rolls of negatives.

Suddenly the main door sprung open behind her. A brilliant projector light blinded her and made her fumble with the clasp of her bag. She spun round and threw up a hand to shade her smarting eyes. As her vision adapted to the bright light, she realised she was standing beside a projected image of herself on the white wall behind.

'Mrs Elizabeth Graham, I believe. Welcome to P.S.I.' said a chilling voice, anything but welcoming in his tone.

The narrow room flooded with the presence of evil. Liz hastily enveloped her psychic body in the white light of divine protection and signed herself with the cross and circle of the rosy cross, refusing to let the sneering mockery of the man behind the projector undermine her faith in her action prayer.

'What, am I royalty now, that I have no anonymity in public?' she demanded, gesturing to the projection of her face on the wall.

He studied the contrasting images before him: the slide of Liz Kirkland three months before her marriage when her Romany appearance was unaffectedly casual; beside the fragile, model-perfect woman standing seven feet away; and wondered how on earth his psychics had foreseen his downfall by such an actress.

'Your image is public property whenever you are in a public place. I have been expecting you.'

'Then you must be more clairvoyant than I am. Who are you?'

Again, the lighting changed. The projector switched off and the room flared with fluorescent light. In the doorway stood an influential man Liz recognised from an article in a business magazine her husband liked to read. His face was distinctive, mature and handsome, with hard dark eyes beneath low brows and a strong chin concealed by a greying beard. Of medium height and thick-set, he dressed well without ostentation in dark grey, and he carried himself with the arrogance of a man who has an unassailable advantage over the world.

'Jonathan Keast! So you have a finger in this pie too!'

Her correct identification was significant to him.

'Let us adjourn to an office to continue this interview,' he ordered with deadly charm: 'After you have returned our negatives.'

She mistook his reserve to be lenience towards her unauthorised presence there and reached for the push-bar on the emergency exit.

'I had been thinking it was about time I left and went home for lunch. I'm inclined to faint if I forget lunch.'

'Must I remind you, Mrs Graham, that you are trespassing on these premises and you have our property in your handbag. You will not be leaving anywhere until I have decided whether or not to call the police.'

His threat was enough to make her concede his advantage. She opened her handbag and replaced one roll of film on the worktop, hoping she would still manage to keep the rest for Alec to see.

'And the other two.'

He was more interested in exerting control over her than retrieving the bait for his improvised trap. Now that the wife of his adversary had fallen unexpectedly into his hands, he had no intention of letting her go until he had assessed her potential value for information, ransom and blackmail.

Liz obediently replaced two more rolls of negatives on the worktop, trying not to think about his miscalculation over the photographs in case he sensed her little victory. She decisively refastened her handbag and walked towards him. He stepped aside to let her pass. Close to him she picked up the masculine sensuality of his presence and felt betrayed by her own body's response.

He escorted her to a spacious wood-panelled office on the first floor. The furniture was large and heavy, and the floor was carpeted, but everything had a functional appearance out of keeping with the sort of office Keast would inhabit. Liz guessed it was the office of his subordinate, the manager of the printing house. She sat down where Keast ordered on the hard-backed chair in front of the desk and watched him warily as he sat opposite her.

'My secretary told me she happened to meet you at Gatwick this morning.'

Liz realised he was trying to disconcert her and hid her alarm at discovering the person behind Terry. She mentally placed her psychic self out of the temporal plane into the river of eternity, out of the reach of the physical world of temptation and pride. It freed her mind to respond without fear.

'So you are the Jon fellow whose name I've heard so much recently.'

She noticed the signet ring on his right hand, which bore the same motif as the logo engraved on Andrew Ferry's tankard, and the badge embroidered on the tie worn by Alec's former friend, Pierre Eve.

'Why did you give our German delegate Rolf Krueger such a dire warning at the airport today?' he demanded.

When she did not answer, he pressed, 'Why are you persecuting my society?'

She looked at him in astonishment. 'Me? Persecuting you? I didn't even know P.S.I. existed until today.'

'Come now! P.S.I. has been in existence for nearly twenty years. We've branches in fourteen countries. You have been a practising occultist for ten of those years. We could not have coexisted in this capital without you having heard of P.S.I.'

His accurate reference to her past took her aback. She struggled to mask it with a challenge.

'Just what was Pierre Eve's relationship to you?'

'You knew our French delegate?'

He was concerned to discover he should have listened to Eve before the Frenchman had run. Her reply confirmed his mistake.

'Only briefly. It was through Pierre that I first met Alec. He tried to sell me some drugs. What happened to him?'

'He's dead. His car collided with a lorry when his brakes failed on his way back to Paris. A sad loss, of course: he betrayed us all.'

Liz gave Keast a double look. The way he had spoken implied that Eve's brakes had failed because he had betrayed them all. She recalled the postcard Alec had received from Beirut shortly after Pierre had left, and realised she was face to face with the writer, JK. Keast saw her dismayed expression and smiled.

'I see we have another idealist here: someone who trespassed on my property to protest about an invasion of privacy. Or did you have some other reason for prying?'

His mockery riled her out of her equanimity.

'You were the one who knew I was coming and set up the picture show. You tell me.'

He smiled more broadly and threatened her by reaching out for the telephone. She realised her mistake and quickly brought her temper back in check.

'Then you're quite happy for me to ask what happened to the pewter tankard,' she threatened in return.

He stared thoughtfully at her, starting to appreciate the danger she posed. He himself had accidentally incurred her involvement by placing Pierre Eve in a position to look for her. And now the death of the actor Andrew Ferry was proving to be a serious mistake too, just as Douglas Angus had warned his headstrong brother Sandy, because it had drawn her in further. So far, by trying to avert the predicted future, all they had done was to bring it upon themselves sooner.

'Why did you come here, Mrs Graham?'

'I was just checking out an address in Andrew Ferry's diary.'

'You knew the actor?'

'He was a friend of Alec's mother. He must have been quite important in your organisation for you to remember him too.'

She gave Keast a brittle smile to emphasise her advantage, glanced at her watch and continued, 'May I suggest you come to a decision whether to report me to the police or send me packing with a flea in my ear. I told my driver to come looking for me here if I didn't return to the car in half an hour, and the time is almost up. If he doesn't find me, he will immediately notify my husband who will go straight to the police to file a complaint for kidnapping. P.S.I.'s involvement in two newsworthy events in less than eighteen hours might be a little unfortunate with the delegates' conference so near.'

He regarded her with a cold expression which made her feel like a small scorpion he would crush underfoot as soon as the opportunity arose. But the time was not yet: she was not valuable enough to keep or to destroy. He could tell from the way she spoke that she had no real understanding of her true situation and knew even less about her husband than he did. He decided to let her go, with enough doubts in her mind about her husband to ensure she would find out what he wanted to know before the day was over.

'You really think you are worth that much to your husband now, Mrs Graham? You could die tomorrow and the control of his father's estate would still be his by Christmas. Dr Graham only chose you for his wife because your background gives you the wisdom not to place too many demands on him.'

'Rivals you may be, but I didn't expect a man of your standing to stoop low enough for such a personal attack. You may not appreciate Alec's finer points but I assure you they are many. Think twice before you slander him again.'

'My apologies, Mrs Graham: I understood your marriage to be one of convenience on both sides. Why else would the gypsy transform herself into the cover girl? Why else does her husband never take her on his business trips? And why does he never tell her anything about his business, even when she asks? Perhaps she loves him enough to live without the truth, but does he love her enough to be honest with her?'

'And are you on such unsure ground, Mr Keast, that you can only give veiled hints? If you have a message for Alec, speak out. If not, let me go.'

His eyes met hers and held her gaze with a look of malevolent warning. 'I have already given my message, Mrs Graham, and it is for you, not your husband. If you tamper with me, you will regret the consequences. Is that understood?'

The intense malice he projected into her green eyes seemed

to have been dredged from the depths of hell. She clutched the crucifix at her neck and struggled to reunite herself with the river of eternity until her panic subsided.

'That is understood,' she said.

He escorted her off the premises. As she stepped with relief into the sultry air outside, the white Oldsmobile drove up to the factory gates to collect her. She climbed gratefully into the back seat. Theo accelerated away at once to take her out of danger. In the rear-view mirror he saw Jonathan Keast standing inside P.S.I.'s doorway watching their departure. Theo knew he would have to warn Alec as soon as possible about his wife's Sunday morning work.

2 : 8

Goldie came out to meet Liz as she arrived back at Briarbank.

'Are you all right, my child?' she demanded, having sensed she had been in danger and feeling contrite for sending her there.

Liz gave her a hug, grateful to have arrived safely home after her encounter with Keast.

'I've made an ass of myself, Goldie. Alec will not be at all amused, and Theo has warned me he will make sure he knows. Is Alec around?'

'No: he drives to the airport to collect Philip. With Andrew dead he is to stay here too. So do not worry - Alec does not like guests and scenes to mix. Now come through and eat your lunch and tell me all about it.'

Goldie propelled Liz into the kitchen and retrieved a salad from the fridge as she continued to talk.

'When we leave the police station Alec is very pleased with you for trying to obey his wishes, and there is no talk of asses then. This happens since?'

Liz nodded. She opened her handbag and passed Goldie the small black book which she had persuaded Theo to hand back to her after his unexpected and forthright lecture on the way home. 'Andrew Ferry's diary, delivered to you as I promised his A.S.M. Jeannie. Andrew asked her to pass the diary on to you just before he died, so you could find out who murdered him. Have you done something like this before?'

'Yes, yes, yes,' Goldie said dismissively: 'When I work with Andrew and Peter Hanson in the all-time epic *Lavinia*, our good friend Ronald Roxburgh is found dead on set one morning. The verdict is suicide; but we prove otherwise - dear Ronald dies for hearing a message not for his ears. Now, tell me what happens.'

Liz smiled at Goldie's impatience and told her all she had done since they had parted company at the police station three hours before, her narrative punctuated by the occasional forkful of salad.

'When we found someone had cleaned out Andrew's apartment too, Jeannie was so upset. And I felt angry, because even the pewter tankard had gone, so it had to be the key. Jeannie thought the tankard and the trouble came from a club called the Psychic Society Incorporated. I looked in the back of the diary and found its address listed there. I also found the Peace and Sincerity Institute listed - the same initials - and I thought an organisation that plays games with its name like that must think it has something to hide. So I tricked Theo into taking me there.'

'And does it have something to hide?'

'Yes. Take a look at these.'

Liz emptied her handbag of the items she had stolen from the darkroom: the photograph, two rolls of negatives, an empty film canister, and a small round tin like a snuffbox decorated with an elaborate red, blue and gold pattern. She opened the little tin out of curiosity. It contained a beige-coloured powder.

'Don't touch that!' Goldie ordered in alarm, knowing what

was in the powder.

Liz obediently put the lid back on the tin and put it in her pocket.

'Why not?'

'Leave that to Alec!'

Goldie picked up one of the rolls of negatives to dismiss the matter and held some of the frames against the light from the window.

'I am not a photographer, but I am right to think these photos are of you, and me, yes?'

Liz nodded. She had looked at them in the car during the embarrassed silence after Theo's lecture.

'And guess who was looking through them in the darkroom - Alec's business rival Jonathan Keast, just about the nastiest man I have ever come across. It was all I could do to get out of there without him calling the police. He said he'd been expecting me. But no-one met me when I arrived, which is why I went in so far. So I guess it must have been a trap, except I told no-one I was going there: I didn't even know myself until I went.'

'Ah, but you deal with people like ourselves, Liz: the ones who see beyond the mask of today. This man you meet is gifted and powerful; and, what is unusual for one of such talent, totally evil.'

'Yes, that is how I sensed him. But how do you know that? Have you met Mr Keast too?'

'So Alec still does not tell you?'

Goldie impatiently put down the roll of film and picked up the small black diary. In an abrupt change of subject she asked, 'Where can I find a Bible?'

Liz felt hurt that Goldie still refused to tell her more, but made no comment as she fetched a Bible from the study. Goldie leafed through the pages of the Old Testament while continuing to speak.

'Every Sunday Andrew writes a text for each day of the

week in his diary. Often he says it is so right for the day. Take his text for today, Lamentations 2, verse sixteen. He reads it tonight and tomorrow keeps its message in his heart...' She paused to read the text, paled and snapped the book shut. Tucking the Bible under her arm, she crossed to the sink and began to fill the coffee percolator.

Liz finished her last few forkfuls of salad watching Goldie in surprise: Goldie rarely ever lifted a finger in the kitchen. She took her empty plate to the sink to rinse it and then slipped the Bible from under Goldie's arm to see what she was trying to hide.

The reference read, *All your enemies rail against you; they hiss, they gnash their teeth, they cry 'We have destroyed her! This is the day we longed for; now we have it; we see it!'*

'I think that is a warning I had a right to know, Goldie. Just as that man at the airport today, Rolf Krueger had the right to know he must change, or die. To tell a man that isn't persecution, is it?'

Goldie turned back to face her.

'It depends how you tell him. Do you think you persecute him?'

'No. But the warning must have come as quite a shock, considering we'd only just met. I had to tell him: his death would be on my conscience if I hadn't. Mr Keast used it to prove his claim I was persecuting P.S.I. I told him I hadn't even heard of the society until today. But afterwards his words did raise my doubts.'

'Yes, and that is all they are said for, to raise doubt. That is how dangerous this man is: with a twist of a word, a movement of the face, he changes all you believe in, to nothing. You must use all your faith to resist him.'

'Alec believes in nothing, but according to Theo he's waging some sort of business war with him.'

'That is for Alec to tell you about: do not ask me again!'

Goldie changed the subject once more as she retrieved two

coffee cups.

'Now, tell me about this Elliot Mayfield who casts horoscopes for your friends' magazine *Helicon*. I think I recognise his ghost writer.'

Liz looked at her in alarm, which made her laugh.

'Your outrageous words cannot hide the way you work, Liz. But I am pleased you find such a discreet way to continue practising your profession. I suspect Alec does know about it though: he lets you keep your secret as long as he can keep all his. So tell me, is this the magazine to feature Sean Cookson, the Irishman who wrote the play for Andrew that you have the party for last night?'

Liz said it was and began to talk about the Print Workshop and Guy and Fran, not realising Goldie was deliberately taking her mind off the morning's events to put her in better spirits for explaining her actions to her husband on his return.

2 : 9

Alec arrived back at Briarbank with Philip shortly after four o'clock. Theo met the black Lincoln in the drive. Alec knew from his expression that something was wrong and took him into the study to discuss the issue in private.

Philip joined Goldie and Liz in the lounge for afternoon tea. Liz was presiding over the tea trolley as the housekeeper Mrs B was away with Sam for the afternoon visiting relatives in the East End. Philip gave Liz an arch smile.

'So what have you been doing today that you should not have been, little Liz?' he asked, settling in an armchair to juggle with a plate of sandwiches and a full cup of tea, and thinking once again that the English have a strange sense of humour.

'It is no joking matter, Philip,' Goldie warned.

'Nothing ever is with Alec,' he returned.

'He does laugh at some things: he's got a very subtle sense

of humour,' Liz protested.

'So do most tyrants!' Philip laughed. 'Look at you both! Like frightened rabbits because the dog is about to bark.'

Goldie started to rebuke him in Greek but heard the study door open. With unexpected speed, she slipped out into the hall and caught hold of Alec's arm to intercept him. He stopped out of family deference, but his cold eyes warned her he resented her interference.

'Alec, before you say any words you regret, remember the fault is mine. I send Liz to find out about Andrew - I ask her to help us avenge his death. She does only as the dutiful daughter, as you do when I ask you. If you tell her all the truth before today, she does not take such risks - it is your fault for not warning her to beware.'

Alec shook her off impatiently.

'Go and look after Philip in the lounge! Liz?'

His wife already stood in the hall, her manner composed and her face serene. Though she would have preferred to avoid a confrontation with her husband after her daunting interview with Keast, she was quite prepared to meet him halfway. Goldie stepped aside to let her pass, sending her telepathic messages of strength and support.

Alec followed his wife into the study and closed the door behind them. Liz picked up a copy of *Helicon* from a chair so that she could sit down at the oak desk, and noticed the *Astro Mountain* page as she threw the magazine aside on a shelf. How right she had been to forecast dissension at home for herself, she thought. Alec sat down opposite her and stared witheringly into her eyes. Though his facial expression showed intense anger, she sensed that behind his mask lurked the more tragic emotions of betrayal and hurt.

'What is the reason for your actions today?' he demanded.

'Exactly what Goldie just told you,' she said, trying to reassure him: 'After you left me at the police station I...'

'How long have you known Keast?' he interrupted.

'A couple of hours?' She struggled not to reply in a way that would escalate their confrontation. 'We met for the first time today. An evil man, I thought. But the name...'

'How much do you know about Keast?'

'Very little: just odd comments of yours on the phone and that magazine article you kept.' Despite herself she began to bite back. 'I do know his first name is Jonathan; and Jon's a name I've heard a little too often recently for you to fob me off with the excuse of business anymore. Why did Theo tell me you and Keast "hate each other's guts"? What has eminent archaeologist Dr Graham got to do with a well-placed satanic social club leader? And what connections did you and he have with the death of Pierre Eve who he claimed "betrayed us all"?'

'Liz, this "satanic social club leader" is a very dangerous man! He is renowned in the European underworld; he thinks nothing of life, and his "social club" P.S.I. is nothing more than a front for his criminal activities. He is feared by all, and it is worth fearing him.'

'That I did come to realise. Throughout our interview he made it very clear who was in control.'

'Then why did you meet him at P.S.I. Chelsea?'

'I didn't arrange to meet him there. It was just an address in Andrew Ferry's diary, a Christian mission or something called the Peace and Sincerity Institute. How was I to know it was Keast's club?'

'Come on, Liz: you aren't that naïve! Theo told me you deliberately withheld the name of the place until it was too late.'

'Of course I did: he wouldn't have taken me otherwise. Your mother sent me on a mission, to find out as much as I could about Andrew Ferry's death, which I did. And for a complete novice in one Sunday lunch time I think I did reasonably well. My one mistake was to walk into Mr Keast's trap; but I did get out of that without any real harm being done, and with a lot of information which you in your great wisdom have refused or omitted to tell me yourself.'

Alec felt relieved that his wife had not deliberately betrayed him to his arch-enemy, but was astonished to find her confidently answering him back for once. He ignored her counter-attack and tried to belittle her newfound self-esteem.

'I have a very good reason for that, Liz. I want to save you from the trouble that always surrounds money. You don't yet appear to realise that when you are married you have to think of someone else as well as yourself. That someone happens to be me. I care enough to protect you, from all the people who would pester you for money or kidnap you....'

'Kidnap me? You must be joking!'

'I am not. Money talks in many circles, influence in others; either can be a motive for kidnap. I know how to handle such problems, but you don't. Despite all my measures to safeguard you, your carefree manner makes you an easy target for any professional. Jonathan Keast was only teasing me today when he toyed with you: he was warning me how easily he could snatch you from my grasp.'

Alec rose from his chair to perch on the edge of the desk, much as a school-master might sit over a wayward child.

'Liz, not everyone is as innocent as you. I love you for that integrity, for your whole attitude towards money and power and prestige as being no more than the necessities they are in the scheme of things. Nothing has changed in you apart from what I wanted you to change, and then only enough to keep me happy and proud of the little Liz I love. So now I'm asking you to change in one last small way. Even though you don't care about our privilege, please at least think about me, the one who loves you. Never put yourself at risk, not for Goldie; not even for me, for I can survive despite the odds because I know the field we're playing in. You don't. You never think badly of people even when they hurt you – your compassion makes you underestimate all too many rogues. Yes, help me in my work when I ask, but keep to your symbolism and your theosophy: leave me to deal with the criminals.'

Alec's homily succeeded in making Liz feel small, but he failed in his intention to rouse her guilt because he still had not answered any of her questions. After her meeting with Keast she was determined to learn the truth from her husband, if only to settle the doubts which his rival had raised in her mind.

'You seem to have a rather unusual view of your colleagues, Alec. What training have you had to deal with criminal archaeologists? And why have you again dodged answering my questions, sidestepping the Keast issue for a sermon on love and marriage? I'm your wife: I have a right to know why you have an evil man like Keast after you. How can you expect me to avoid places like the factory in Cremorne Grove when you tell me less than nothing about it all? I've had enough! I want to be trusted: I want to know. If you won't tell me, I'll have to go and find someone who will.'

Alec stared at her, lost for words, torn between the equal horrors of having her discuss their variance outside the family or making his own admission about the past. Logic told him the truth would be better served by her hearing the story from him first, but though he knew she would not deliberately scorn him for his confession, he was still apprehensive about her reaction. He took a deep breath and plunged in.

'You ask me why I hate Keast? He murdered my brother Kevin, and through him my father.'

'Murdered? How?' she gasped. She remembered the vision of the dear one in lilies she had seen around Alec when she had read his Tarot cards the day they met, and understood it at last. She held his hand to reassure him and encouraged him to continue.

'It was heroin. I watched him die...'

He broke off, struggling to control his emotions as he released the memories repressed for so many years because of their power to hurt. Head low, he continued, 'Do you know what heroin does to a man? How he'll sell his soul for another shot, he'll do anything to get the money...'

'Oh yes: I've seen too many living corpses not to know,' she said, recalling the suffering addicts she had seen in the recovery group at Father Jay's chapel.

'A living death - how true. Father didn't realise. He told Kevin to pull himself together and get back to his studies. Kevin said he needed more money. God, that argument - it haunts me still. Goldie and I were in the lounge. Father refused him. There was a scuffle. I ran into the study to stop them. He had his hands round his throat - throttling him to get money. I threw him off - he ran away... But Father was already dead - heart attack brought on by the shock. It was all hushed up. And within the month Kevin was dead too, of an overdose. I never felt so alone in all my life...'

He pulled away to stand at the window so that he could hide the pain he still felt. She ran to his side and put her arm around his shoulders to comfort him.

'At least it's all over now.'

'But it's not over!' he cried, pulling away once more: 'Every day it happens again and again. All those young people who join P.S.I. to dabble in the safe edge of the black arts, they are being drawn into it too just as Kevin was, with Keast's mystic preparations for meditative experience...'

'You mean this stuff?'

Liz produced the little tin of beige powder from her pocket and dropped it in Alec's hand. He sat down at the desk in dismay.

'Where did you get this?'

'I picked it up at P.S.I. Chelsea. Perhaps Mr Keast was not as prepared for me as he claimed.'

She sat opposite him again.

'Do Goldie and Philip know about all this?'

'Yes: Philip was especially close to Kevin - they were about the same age. They did everything together; until Kevin got embroiled in that damn' club of Keast's. It broke Philip's heart to see the change in him. I can still see him swearing vengeance over his grave. These past eight years Philip and I have tried again and again to bring Keast to justice, but we fail every time. So often we have been within inches of catching him red-handed, only for him to escape us yet again. It's not just the influence he has in all the right places: his life seems to be charmed. Take this Easter - Philip heard on the grapevine that Keast was making moves in the Middle East. We investigated and found he had completely restructured P.S.I.'s Lebanese branch with his usual heavy-handed style under the guise of Moslem-Christian disturbances – another four dead.'

'Which is why you disappeared to the Lebanon after getting that postcard about a two-way transmitter?'

'Yes. You weren't meant to see that card. I arrived in Beirut to find Keast had given us a runner: he was actually up the coast sorting out a Turkish drugs supplier for fouling up a shipment. I flushed him out for Philip to tail, but he gave us the slip in Amsterdam and once again we lost the connection between him and his deeds.'

'So you came home and we got engaged....'

'And I found Keast's secretary Teresa Carter trying to befriend you through Bethany. Pierre Eve had clearly been right when he told me P.S.I. has some talented psychics - they must have warned Keast about Philip and me and advised him to get back at us through you. Your meeting with Keast at P.S.I. Chelsea only confirms this: where we had failed to track him down for two months, you made a spur-of-the-moment decision on the evidence presented to you and walked straight into his clutches. Yes, you are psychic too, but second sight will not save you from the evil of a man like Keast. He knows I'm after his blood and he'll do all he can to stop me; so I don't want you getting in the way. I must therefore insist you stay out of things from now on. I have given Theo strict orders to make sure you do nothing rash: if necessary, he will even restrain you by force. So forget Jonathan Keast and Teresa Carter and P.S.I. Become the dutiful wife, and leave me to avenge all the death and the suffering that bastard has scattered in his wake. Go back to your cards and your charts and your pen, and leave the killing to those with the guns.'

Liz sat staring at Alec, stunned to have learned how much he had hidden from her, and how little she had really found out without his help. But still there were discrepancies she did not understand. She ventured to have these answered while he was being so expansive.

'So Goldie is not your real mother, and Philip is not your real brother.'

'No: Goldie and Arthur were close friends of my parents. When my mother died having Kevin Goldie adopted us, in a manner of speaking. She had just had Philip, and we all grew up together, an unconventional family with two part-time fathers: Arthur was always away making films, and my father was always away on business, making his fortune with the specialised laminating process he invented. When Arthur died five years ago Goldie retired to their villa in Greece and Philip took over the management of the estate, turning half of it into a wine empire. What little spare time he isn't chasing Keast, he spends seducing his female employees.'

'You mean, the first time we met, he wasn't trying to vet me for the position of your wife at all - he was just attempting another conquest?'

Alec gave a little smile and sat back on the edge of the desk near her.

'No, Liz, though I can't blame you for thinking that. A clause in my father's will stipulated that his estate would be held in trust until Kevin and I married partners who met with the approval of the rest of the "family". That is why I have so many more business commitments since we married - my father's estate has come out of trust and is now completely in my control.'

'Which explains that a bit differently to the way Mr Keast put it today.'

Liz stood up and put her hands on her husband's shoulders. 'Oh, Alec, at last I understand why you find it so hard to trust me. Everyone you've really loved, you've lost. Only time can prove that won't be the case with me. At least be assured of this: as far as I'm concerned, our marriage is for life, and I intend giving you a wonderful new family to make up a little for the loving family you've lost.'

She kissed him with a warm desire which eclipsed all his hurt and painful memories. For the first time in his life he felt released from the shadows which had turned all his past happiness to ashes. He responded to her embrace with a warmth she had not felt in him before. She slid her arms under his jacket to draw him closer in a more passionate kiss.

Suddenly she recoiled: her right had touched the unyielding metal of a gun concealed in a shoulder holster beneath his jacket. She looked up into his face in dismay. Once again, she perceived the psychic image of the sword within him which her love had blinded her to since their first month together; and she realised his cold intellectualism was no act but a potent force which he was deliberately cultivating to his detriment.

'You must have one helluva grudge, Alec. What do you intend doing with that?' she asked in a low uncertain voice.

'Pay back the men who killed my brother and my father, who killed Ferry and Eve and those people in the Lebanon, and who will mercilessly go on killing until they are stopped.'

'Do you think that one clip of bullets, a few little bits of lead will stop them and the evil behind them? You hypocrite! What right do you have to do to them what you condemn them for?'

He put her aside and walked away again to the window to gain thinking time before he turned back to answer her.

'I have every right: I have a special licence and a commission to bring these men to justice. They have ruined hundreds of lives. They think nothing of murder, and just because you read Tarot cards won't prevent you from being killed by them too.'

'But Alec, it's a crime to take a life: your resentment and your past griefs would make you as much a murderer as they are.'

'Oh, no: I could never be as sadistic as those mercenary bastards!'

'It's not a matter of degree, Alec: forget the legality of it all. When you take someone's money or their home, or you kidnap their child or imprison them, you're taking something that can be returned; but when you take a life you can never give it back, no matter how much you may regret it: you're not God.'

A smile stole over Alec's face - he always found his wife's soap-box speeches amusing. He easily countered her with her own words from a previous occasion which he knew would make her see red.

'But maybe I will be brought to regret my crimes because liberal little Liz believes it her duty to save people like Keast and me, not kill them...'

'Don't you patronise me, you pompous, stuck up old woman! You...'

Philip's laughter from the open study door interrupted them. Liz looked nervously across at Alec and knew from his clenched hands and narrowed eyes that he was very angry again.

'Forgive me, Liz, Alec,' Philip apologised as he came into the room. 'Mrs B asked me to tell you that she is back to make dinner, but Sam has been delayed and will phone later...'

Their uncomprehending faces at his unexpected message made him laugh all the more.

'I am truly sorry, Liz,' he said, struggling to check himself, 'but this is the first time I have heard anyone slander Alec and live to tell the tale. Not only did you call him a murderer and a hypocrite, but best of all, a pompous stuck up old woman too. And in my opinion, you are quite correct.'

'Philip!' Goldie scolded, following him in. She saw from their expressions that she needed to calm the situation and delivered a modified version of a speech she had once spoken in a short-run play. 'No matter what we are, our good Lord makes each one of us for a purpose. God knows that a world full of Lizes would be a world full of ideals and little action; while a world full of Alecs would be a cold silent world. But He also knows that without Lizes and Alecs, and without Philips and Goldies and Andrews and Jonathan Keasts the world is dead. Man needs the idealist, the one who acts, the leader, the follower and the goad of evil, for each of us to find our true potential. The whole universe is a vast machine in balance: who are we to upset that harmony by criticising the individual parts? Ours is to accept, to try our best guided by our consciences to make the world a better place for our fellow men...'

'While to maintain the balance men like Keast do their best to make it worse?' Alec scoffed.

'Does he?' Liz demanded, to challenge Alec's cynicism rather than develop a relevant argument: 'True, he's abusing people in his greed to acquire power and wealth, but maybe he hasn't yet worked out that the Devil's way is second best, the easy option. He must believe that what he's doing will make the world a better place for him and his kind, or he wouldn't be doing it; just as you clearly believe the world as it is, is a better place for you and your kind or you wouldn't be defending it.'

'You must be joking! That man throws people like you on the scrap heap every day with stuff like this!' Alec exclaimed, pushing the little tin of beige powder towards her across the desktop.

Philip swiftly reached past her and picked up the tin before she could touch it. He inspected its contents closely, the laughter gone from his smiling eyes.

'Where did you get this from?' he asked them both in concern.

'I picked it up accidentally in the darkroom at P.S.I. Chelsea. What is it?'

'Usually run of the mill herbal tranquillisers and stimulants you can buy over the counter from any good chemist for a few pence,' Philip replied: 'This tin with the blue line in the red, has an added extra which puts the price up and places it under the counter. Not so pleasant dreams all round in here. No good raiding the place now though: it will have had a complete spring clean since Liz's visit.'

'Then you don't think they meant me to find this when I was there?'

'Oh, yes: Keast certainly meant you to have this,' Philip said: 'That's how evil the man really is: he knows that with your past, all you would need to do is to sample the powder to find out what it is, and you'd be right back where you were seven years ago when you first joined Father Jay's recovery group.'

Goldie saw the dismay on Liz's face at Philip's understanding of her past and stepped in to ask, 'Then the photos Liz finds there and brings home: Mr Keast wanted her to have them too?'

'What photos?' Alec demanded.

Philip handed him the negatives and the print Liz had brought home with her while Liz answered him.

'Pictures of Goldie and me at Gatwick Airport this morning. Mr Keast caught me as I was putting the films in my bag. I asked him why he had invaded my privacy like that. He said much the same thing in return and threatened me with the police. He also said my image is public property whenever I'm in a public place.'

Philip saw Alec's eyes flash as he heard his wife's innocent repetition of Keast's subtle threat. Knowing how Alec could react to any potential as well as actual violation of his property, Philip touched his right forearm, cautioning him to exercise restraint.

'Keast could only have been trying to turn Liz's surprise visit to his advantage, Alec. He could not have known that Andrew Ferry's diary was still in existence after everything else had gone, let alone that a stagehand would give the diary to your wife who would look at the addresses in the back, choose one at random and go straight to P.S.I. Chelsea from the dead man's apartment.'

'Is this true, Liz?' Alec asked her.

'Here is the proof: the address in the back,' Goldie said, showing him the diary entry.

'It's only partly true: I didn't choose the address at random,' Liz confessed: 'You were right about the initials, Alec; but I wasn't lying because I hadn't tied up the club with Keast. I tied the initials up with the number plate on the powder blue Jag and the engraved motif on Andrew Ferry's tankard. It was the A.S.M. Jeannie who put me on to P.S.I. as a club when she said Equity never worked like that. When I got to the place in Chelsea, I found what seemed to be a New Age print house. But then I saw the signet ring on Mr Keast's left hand, and I wished you had told me about it all instead of leaving me to find out for myself.'

'I didn't even realise you still wanted to know. And I don't remember Andrew having an engraved tankard when we met him. Why, he would have to be a member to have had one of those.'

'You can say that, Alec? After you asked Mr Ferry in my presence, "Has Sandy Angus been up to his tricks again?" Of course Andrew was a member, and you knew it. And so did that policeman Marner who knew so much about him despite it only being the natural death of an old man on the way to hospital after a heart attack. The tapestry is gold from one side, but quick-silver on the other: which angle should I look at it - truth or fiction? And you didn't realise I still wanted to know?'

'Calm yourself, Liz: your emotional response is clouding your vision,' Goldie warned. 'Alec, my friend Andrew never touches drugs or uses violence: he makes many mistakes in his life, but those are not two of them. So why does he join this club, which you say is only a front for Mr Keast's evil?'

Philip sensed his mother was already displeased to learn

what Liz had just discovered and knew she would like what he had to say even less. He took hold of her hands in an attempt to placate her as he answered her question.

'Mother, I have a confession to make. Andrew Ferry joined P.S.I. because I asked him to, after Alec and I realised what was being sold in some of these little tins. We can only guess at the events leading up to his death, but it seems that while Alec and Liz were away on honeymoon in June and I was busy in the vineyards, Andrew heard someone threaten either Liz or Alec. With no-one else to turn to he took the information straight to the police, where Inspector Marner somehow picked up the case. Marner reassured Andrew they had dealt with the matter, but he went straight to Keast about the betrayal behind Andrew's back.'

'Then when Liz and I met Andrew yesterday evening, he could tell from what we said that Marner had not passed his warning on to us. So when I told him about the Angus twins he mentioned the threats to his life.'

'But the Jon boy threat against Elizabeth Graham was common knowledge long before June,' Liz objected: 'Guy's *Iron Fist* reporter tipped me off almost a month before. That was why Mr Keast sent his personal secretary to befriend me, wasn't it? Only I couldn't believe that the beautiful Miss Carter found my rather poor article about fortune telling to pad out the *Iron Fist* so wonderful that she had to meet me but backed off from having her Tarot cards read.'

'You knew all this and didn't tell me?' Alec demanded, shocked.

'Are you so transparent yourself?' Goldie asked and gave a harsh little laugh. 'Don't worry, boys: now we understand the problem, Liz and I are content to sit on the side-lines while you two have the fun and take the risks; but do not underestimate us again. We may ask no questions, but we still find our answers; and our gifts would be put to far better use helping you both. Then my dear friend Andrew would still be playing the lead in

Sunset tonight.'

'We don't know that,' Liz contradicted.

Goldie waved her silent and glared at Alec and Philip to make sure they appreciated their responsibility for the outcome through their manipulation of the events. Had only Liz been accusing him Alec would have told her she was wrong to blame him for Keast's actions; but he knew Goldie would not accept such glib rationalisation. He felt forced to back down from her challenge.

'I must prepare for when Sam reports in,' he said, and stalked out of the study.

Philip excused himself and followed him out. Goldie shut the door behind them and sat down with Liz at the heavy oak desk. At last she could talk freely with her about Alec's past and set the record straight. As always, she had a great deal to say.

2 : 10

Sam phoned Alec shortly before ten that evening. As Alec had earlier been accused of concealing important facts, he took the call in the lounge so that Goldie and Liz could hear what was said. They learnt little because Sam did most of the talking. Alec noted down an address in the East End with the promise he would go straight there and finished the call.

'The clue about the third man paid off, Philip: Sam's tracked him down to a pub near the old south bank docks,' he said.

'What clue about the third man is this?' Goldie asked.

'It was something Liz said,' Philip replied, glancing at Alec to check whether he should continue.

'But I said there were two of them, not three,' Liz objected.

'Yes,' Alec agreed: 'You saw two people in the car - the Angus twins - and you also saw a third man leave the theatre and get in with them. We checked with the stage doorman: he gave us a description of a man sounding like Douggie Angus's former gangland pal Joe Watson.'

'I still don't see why the Angus twins let themselves be seen that close to a murder when it wasn't an emergency,' Philip said.

'Perhaps it was,' Liz said: 'Maybe they discovered we were going to see Mr Ferry at the theatre and went to collect their accomplice before we turned up. They'd be confident that without that connection Mr Ferry's heart attack would look natural. Only Jeannie said otherwise and Marner was quick to stifle that complaint.'

'Perhaps, Liz. That's what we are about to find out,' Alec said.

He left the lounge to collect some things from the study but stopped in the hall on hearing a loud knock at the front door. Suspicious of an unexpected late visitor, he opened the door himself. On the doorstep stood Bethany, reeking of alcohol and very upset. She pushed her way in demanding to see Liz at once in private.

Liz hastily directed her into the dining room before Alec could say how tired he was getting of her friend's drunken excesses. She closed the door and guided her into a seat by the oak refectory table. Bethany asked for a drink.

'You've already been drinking quite heavily, haven't you?'

'Not really. Terry came round and we sunk a couple of bottles of claret,' Bethany minimised, her speech slurred.

'How can that solve your problems, Beth? All it leaves you with is a few pounds less in your purse and a sore head in the morning.'

'Not this time. These are just the goodbyes: you know, go round everyone and tell them what you really think of them and say goodbye and never go back; and then you'll all be sorry. Goodbye! Have you got a drink?'

'Not here, no. I've given up clouding my senses with alcohol.'

'Bully for you! Liz, I just can't take any more. I got this letter, you see: from a friend, it said. With a photo of Mike, and this other girl. I phoned you but Mrs King said you were out so I called Terry. She came over with a couple of bottles. But someone told Daddy I had a gay girlfriend in my flat; so he came round and chased her out and threw me across the room. And he said all these horrid things that made me scream shut up. He told me, Liz: how Alec phoned him and asked him if getting rid of Mike was worth a sculpture; and all the sordid details I didn't want to hear. And then the pieces fit.'

She fumbled in her pocket for the photograph, but noticed her friend's expression and changed tack.

'You aren't listening, are you, Liz! You don't care a jot about what I'm going through.'

'You know that's not true, Bethany! I just have a few problems of my own tonight; but that doesn't mean I don't care. A friend of the family has just died - that actor we met last night - and I've had an argument with Alec, and I'm not allowed to go anywhere alone anymore because I might get kidnapped by one of Terry's colleagues. So maybe you're not so badly off as you think.'

Bethany nodded knowingly, easily taking offence at Liz's words because of the indoctrination she had received with the two bottles of claret.

'You're having me on, aren't you - you don't care tuppence about what I'm going through. Don't you see, Liz - I know! Terry said I'd be able to tell by your reaction - if you tried to get out of things it meant you're too ashamed to face me. Fair enough: if that's the way you treat your friends, I'll go home and tell Terry all she wants to know about you, and then I'll chuck myself off the balcony. And I hope her friend does murder you!'

At that point Bethany had intended to slam the photograph down in front of Liz, but she had not yet managed to free it from her jacket pocket. Liz quickly spoke while she still fumbled.

'Bethany, what rubbish is that dangerous woman filling your addled brain with?'

'It's not just Terry, Liz: the photo was quite clear too - the girl Mike was with was you!'

Bethany tossed the photograph at Liz and fled from the dining room. Liz chased after her into the hall, pleading with her to stop. Bethany opened the front door and turned back in the doorway to face her with a parting shot while her line of escape was clear.

'I didn't want to believe it, Liz; but what else can I think? Mike, I was learning to face; Daddy, I can cope with; but my best friend double-crossing me...'

She turned away in tears and ran out into the night, slamming the door behind her. Liz wrenched the door open again and called out to her.

'It's not true, Beth! Come back!'

She leapt forward to follow her, but before she could cross the threshold Theo caught her by the waist and pulled her back. He resolutely closed the front door again with his free hand while she struggled indignantly against his strong grip. Once she was safe, he released her. She was about to protest at her treatment when she saw Alec standing in the dining room doorway and realised in horror that he was holding the photograph Bethany had left.

'It isn't true, Alec! I didn't do it. That's the last thing I would have done,' she pleaded, terrified that his jealousy would blind him to the facts.

Alec stood beneath the bright central light in the hall to inspect the photograph more closely. It was a close-up of Liz and Mike in a wood about to embrace, her left hand on his right shoulder with her wedding and engagement rings in clear view. Alec knew it had to be a forgery because of the circumstances shown in the picture, but at first he could not see any tell-tale signs of editing as the photographer had misted the image to conceal them.

'Didn't do what?' he demanded, teasing his wife with an impassive face.

'Go with Mike! I couldn't stand him; and I don't blame Bethany's father at all for getting him to go, though I didn't like your part in it. But as for me going with him...'

'Of course you didn't, dear,' Alec agreed, realising from her protests that his teasing was too severe. He explained, 'This picture is a composite of two re-photographed. The one of you could only have been taken since we married, but since then you haven't been out of my sight or Theo's long enough for anything like this to happen.'

'But Alec, Bethany is going to throw herself off her balcony over these lies!'

'She won't, Liz: she hasn't got the courage. You should be more concerned about who set her up, and why.'

'I think you'll find it was Mr Keast, Doctor,' Theo said: 'Miss Carter's car was parked just round the corner all the time Miss Broome was 'ere, and two cars drove off past our drive right after she left.'

Liz paled to discover how close she had been to danger had Theo not stopped her, and how vulnerable she really was. Chastened, she returned with Alec to the lounge and the comforting company of Goldie and Philip. Goldie demanded to know what the fuss had been about. Alec showed her the photograph and explained what had happened.

'So we have discovered one of the special skills of Keast's photographer at P.S.I. Chelsea,' Philip said, looking at the picture over his mother's shoulder.

With Keast attacking so close to home, Alec delayed no further before going out with Philip to collect Sam, and took Liz with him too for her protection. Goldie declined a late-night drive into the East End with the excuse of needing to make some phone calls which she knew Alec would prefer her doing while he was not there. Alec promptly agreed but took the unusual precaution of leaving Theo behind to look after Goldie and the housekeeper while he left with both Liz and Philip.

As the black Lincoln cruised northwards through the night-lit city streets, the clouds which had been gathering through the day broke into rain. Liz curled up on the front seat and rested her head on Alec's shoulder while he drove. Philip watched them from the back seat, wondering how Alec had found a wife who loved him so much she even took pleasure in a depressing night drive through rain-washed derelict streets because she was at his side. Why did he not put his left arm round her shoulders in return, he wondered, and realised to his surprise that he was jealous of Alec for his good fortune in finding such a gem among the pebbles where he himself had always found the pebbles among the gems.

Their journey ended in a region of warehouses crossed by a maze of deserted back streets around some disused docks off the Thames. Alec parked the Lincoln in the shadows between the beams of two streetlamps and turned off the engine. A few minutes later Sam stepped out of a doorway into the harsh white light of the streetlamp ahead and beckoned to them to follow him. He looked strangely unreal to Liz with his streaming leather trench coat and brimmed hat in the pouring rain and the poorly lit street. Was that because Alec was trying to cut a figure for Philip's benefit, she wondered, or because the other world was trying to communicate with her again?

Sam guided the Lincoln into a sheltered service alley beside a disused warehouse and drew two heavy doors across the lane behind them to conceal the limousine from the road. He bent down by the driver's door. Alec opened his window for him.

'You're too late, Dr Graham; but if you want a look I'll take you over. With this rain, you can't mistake what 'appened,' he said.

'What about Liz?' Alec asked.

'She doesn't 'ave to go up close.'

Sam led the way across the courtyard to the brick-built warehouse and went inside through some battered double doors.

Philip hurried in after him. Alec slid his left arm round Liz's waist and followed them more cautiously. She sensed his concern that they might be walking into an ambush but knew his fears were unfounded. As they entered the warehouse the lights came on, making Alec flinch and spin round. He relaxed again to see not a foe but Philip at the switches, trying the lights because he wanted to see the marks on the floor in a stronger light than Sam's torch.

The tracks over the dusty floorboards stood out plainly as dark patches on light grey, still wet in the damp neglected building. The tyre marks and footprints headed across the floor toward a pile of rags and rubbish by the far wall. The evidence told a brief tale which Sam's commentary extended as they stood inside the door and visualised what had taken place.

'It was Joe Watson the doorman saw,' Sam grimly confirmed. 'I caught up with 'im in a pool hall up the road. We potted a few balls. Then we went outside for a chat. Joe said Ferry shopped Sandy and Douggie Angus to the police when 'e found out they intended doing mischief to a Liz Graham they were looking for, before she did mischief to P.S.I. Another member. D.I. Marner, saw Ferry at the station and lost the complaint after tipping off Keast who passed it on to the Angus twins to deal with. It's like a matter of honour to the twins, but Ferry didn't disappear as planned 'cause 'e 'ad the luck of the Devil. So Douggie called in a little debt from 'is old mate Joe Watson who's been known to play chemist's assistant to Hendrik Gerber; and Ferry's dying even as you're inviting 'im over to Briarbank for tea.'

The story did not seem new to Liz. While Sam spoke on, she stepped round the edge of the floor keeping near the wall, to take a closer look at the sort of rubbish which had two pairs of footprints running to it but only one pair coming back.

'It just so 'appens that the pay-off is tonight, but when Sandy and Douggie come to call, there's Joe 'aving a chat with 'is old mate Sam, only Sam ain't there no more and Douggie looks pretty mad. So Joe nipped off with Douggie at 'is 'eels and Sandy's behind in the Jag. They lost 'im for a while so Douggie got in the Jag, but then they spotted 'im again running in 'ere so they drove in after 'im and knifed 'im.'

Sam belatedly realised where Liz was heading and called out, 'So I wouldn't take a look, ma'am: it's not a pretty sight,' before he concluded more softly, 'I could've sworn it was Sandy at the wheel; but there's no mistaking it: that's Sandy's hallmark.'

Liz moved aside some of the rags in the pile of bloody rubbish and uncovered Joe Watson's body, his torso viciously mutilated but his terrified face untouched. She paused in silent prayer for him. The men though she had frozen in shock and went to pull her away. As they reached her she returned her thoughts to the material world and assured them she was all right.

'That's the fourth face identified: the second death I dreamt about last night. At least he's at rest,' she said, and turned to walk away again, sensing it was time for them to leave.

'Who else did you see?' Philip demanded, chasing after her, leaving Sam and Alec to cover up the body again.

She turned at the door, reluctant to answer him but for his insistence.

'Rolf Krueger and Douggie Angus.'

'Krueger and one of the Angus twins?' he corrected with a one-sided smile.

'No, Philip,' she insisted: 'Douggie Angus - just as Sam said about Sandy, there's no mistaking his hallmark. Come on, we should get going before we are caught here.'

She walked outside to the Lincoln. The three men hurried out after her, shutting off the lights as they left. Soon the black limousine was cruising homeward through the rain-washed backstreets with Alec at the wheel. While his car waited at a dimly lit junction to re-join the main road, a police car raced past with siren screaming, heading in the direction from which they had come. Liz nodded knowingly. Philip watched her by the passing light of the streetlamps and again wondered how Alec had managed to find and keep such a gem.

2 : 11

Liz woke much later than usual next morning. She lay still for a while, savouring the luxury of having all the double bed to herself and enjoying the memory of Alec's more relaxed love-making the night before. Distant voices elsewhere in the house spurred her to get up. She threw back the curtains to see an overcast day and heavy rain. With a sigh for the departing summer she showered and dressed in an autumnal weight long-sleeved black dress.

Goldie broke off from her monologue to the housekeeper as Liz entered the kitchen and gave her a bright greeting. She refused Mrs B's offer to cook her something for breakfast and poured herself a mug of coffee which she sat at the kitchen table to drink.

'No breakfast, my precious?' Goldie enquired, hoping for a family reason.

'I feel a bit muzzy: slept too heavily,' she replied with a yawn.

'And why are you dressed in black again, my precious? Always, always in black? Tcha! Alec should have turned your head away from that corpse.'

'It was my choice to look, Goldie, and I felt more settled after I had seen his face. Despite the dream I couldn't have done anything to save him: he'd already made his choice for destruction. Where's Alec?'

'He takes Philip to a policeman friend about Detective Inspector Marner. Theo and Sam work on the lawn-mower while waiting for Sleeping Beauty to waken. Mrs B tiptoes around here for fear of disturbing you. And me? I feel bored. I say to myself, Goldie, you go on the shopping spree. Do you wish to come with me? I hear you say Croydon is good.'

Liz had experienced enough shopping sprees with Goldie to know Sam and Theo would be as grateful as herself should she dissuade her from that idea.

'I was rather hoping to go around to Bethany's and explain that photograph business to her. Though with Theo in tow, I'm worried she'll think I'm trying the strong-arm touch. Perhaps you could help. Bethany knows you believe in fair play. Maybe we could all have lunch together, at the restaurant on the common.'

Goldie beamed with approval to hear Liz resign herself so readily to Alec's precautions, for she sensed that all would not go as expected for Liz that day.

'Of course Goldie reunites the friends, little Liz. Do not worry that you have lost Bethany. Last night you have the nervous stress, your words are tired and hasty. Now you are calmer, you can explain. You also accept now the things Alec insists upon only for your safety.'

'I accept them because Alec loves me enough to make them, not because I believe in them. Do you really think Jonathan Keast is only having a go at me because he's trying to get back at Alec?'

'But yes,' Goldie lied: 'Mr Keast is a man whose only interest is himself, his safety and increase. Now he interests himself in you, yet you cannot hurt him. But your husband can, and your brother-in-law can. So he tries to get at them through you. So Alec alters the odds: if Theo keeps with you, Mr Keast must deal with you both and so will not try. So I urge you, throw away these fears.'

Liz nodded and finished her coffee but still felt unconvinced. She poured herself a second mug and turned back to explain.

'I'm sorry, Goldie: I just can't forget that Bible quote of Andrew Ferry's; read last night to be borne in mind today. I've been threatened; two men are already dead; and the text that is always so right says *we have destroyed her.*'

'Tcha! I hope to myself you do not remember that. Never worry, little Liz: God is stronger than all the evil men in the world put together - God can put an end to them all just like this!' She snapped her fingers. 'But God doesn't need to: all the evil men in this world destroy themselves. The ill-feeling Mr Keast has for you and Alec is pickling him in vinegar; but do you feel anything now, hien? Just a little worry that you are foolish to keep; but no deep wounds in the back from his knife, no broken bones from his threats, no sleepless nights from his plots. Come, you silly child; let us go to Bethany's and forget this blue mood.'

They left Briarbank in the white Oldsmobile half an hour later, with Sam driving and Theo beside him in the front passenger seat. The rain was easing off as they arrived at Westfield House, shortly before midday. Liz strolled along the rowan-lined asphalt path to the apartment block with Theo behind her, leaving Goldie with Sam as he turned the limousine ready to drive on to the restaurant. While Liz was climbing the carpeted stairs to apartment nine, a prickly feeling climbed her back.

'It's awfully quiet,' she remarked to Theo.

'Some people do 'ave to work on Monday mornings,' he replied lightly, but inwardly he too felt uneasy.

They arrived on the third-floor landing to find the door to Bethany's apartment open and smoke clouding her hall. Theo pushed Liz out of the way and ran inside, alert to other possible dangers besides fire. He followed the smoke to the kitchen and found a flaming piece of toast beneath the grill which he quickly extinguished in the sink. Liz followed him into the kitchen, but glanced through the serving hatch and saw the chaos in Bethany's lounge. She cried out in surprise.

'What's up?' Theo demanded, his right hand hovering near his jacket lapel.

'The mess! Even in her worst drinking bouts, Bethany never left things like that,' Liz replied, pointing through the hatch to the riot of papers, books, and records scattered across the room.

She hurried through to put things back but stopped after she had replaced the telephone receiver when she heard what sounded like a scream from outside. As she stepped out onto the balcony and looked out over the neighbouring buildings to trace the cry, she heard it again: a muffled scream somewhere below her, coming from the garage access drive at the back of Westfield House. Diagonally below her a powder blue Jaguar with four occupants stood with its engine running. In the back seat a man struggled with Bethany, fighting to hold her down.

'Theo! Bethany's outside, down in the drive. Some men have got her in a car like PS 1!'

'They've snatched 'er! Follow me!'

They raced back out of the apartment to the waiting Oldsmobile. As Theo leapt into the passenger seat beside Sam, the Jaguar shot out of the service drive onto the road. Theo ordered Sam to follow while Liz joined Goldie in the back. Before she could shut her door, Sam spun the limousine around the corner onto the road in pursuit, making her almost slide out again.

'What is happening?' Goldie complained.

Sam threw the speeding limousine round a sharp right turn to keep the Jaguar in sight, flinging Goldie hard against her door. Liz clung onto Theo's seat-back to steady herself and kept her eyes on the fast-moving tail-plate of PS 1.

'They've kidnapped Bethany in the car in front! We mustn't let them get away!'

'But this is no good! This is a plot. They leave at just the right moment for us to follow, so we follow!'

The Jaguar turned abruptly off the main road down a side street, and the limousine promptly followed. Goldie slid along the back seat and crushed Liz against her door.

'They wouldn't leave toast burning for dramatic effect,'

Liz said once she had regained her breath.

'They could've, if they used the back fire escape,' Theo replied.

The Jaguar led the limousine through several miles of back-streets before joining the main road crossing the Thames by Wandsworth Bridge. As they drove over the river Liz pointed out the Chelsea Flour Mills to her right and realised they were being led back to the Peace and Sincerity Institute. Concerned, Sam and Theo tersely agreed tactics in low voices.

The two cars turned right and right again, and came out once more in the drab grey industrial avenue of Cremorne Grove. The Jaguar swiftly turned off into the side entrance of the Institute. The factory gates swung shut behind it. Sam brought the limousine to a halt a factory block further along on the opposite side of the road. Theo leapt out of the car with his right hand under his left lapel and dashed across the road behind the cover of a passing lorry. He disappeared from sight through the main entrance into the reception area of P.S.I. Chelsea's offices.

Everything went quiet outside. The Institute gazed back across the street, drab and impassive. Two factory chimneys nearby billowed plumes of condensing steam which were reflected by the drying puddles in the gutters. Disconsolate workers hurried blindly along the concrete pavements through the aesthetic wilderness of their working environment. Goldie watched them with an expression of bored impatience.

'I think I take my shopping spree tomorrow.'

'At least Bethany didn't throw herself off the balcony.'

'Giddown!' Sam ordered, diving below the level of the dashboard.

As Liz and Goldie ducked a bullet smashed through the rear windscreen and embedded in Sam's sun visor. A second shot hit a moving target outside. Squealing brakes ended with the crash of metal on brick as an articulated lorry jack-knifed and collided with a low wall, coming to rest behind the limousine amid a debris of bricks and cement. The passers-by vanished from the pavement and the street became instantly, eerily deserted.

Sam engaged gear to drive off, only to have to swerve to avoid a bread van which reversed out of a factory in front of the limousine. The van stalled, blocking the road. He disengaged the engine again and ducked back down behind the dashboard.

'Remind me to ask Alec for a car with bullet-proof windows for Christmas,' Liz joked with laboured levity.

'Ask for one that can fly too: we're trapped,' Sam said. 'Your only way of escape is into Calatex, the factory opposite P.S.I. Take a quick look to get your bearings, but be careful.'

Liz cautiously peered over the back seat to weigh up their surroundings. Goldie took one look at the distances involved and turned back in disgust.

'I stay in the car. That is hopeless.'

'I'll have a go, Sam, if you think it's the only option,' Liz said, and looked sideways at Goldie who had huffed in disdain. 'Don't worry: I've got long lifelines on both hands and I said my prayers this morning.'

'Is that what you want me to tell Alec?' Goldie icily replied.

Sam checked the breech of his Smith & Wesson revolver while giving Liz her instructions. He got out of the limousine by the front passenger door ready to cover her flight. Once he was in position Liz picked up her handbag and scrambled out. On his command she sprinted along the pavement towards Calatex as fast as her elegant court shoes would allow.

A security guard left P.S.I.'s factory gates to cut Liz off, distracting them from noticing the driver of the bread van as he left his vehicle and headed towards the limousine. Sam fired across the guard's path until he headed back to the safety of P.S.I. Goldie realised the van driver's intentions and cried out to Sam in warning. He turned too late: the man smashed the heels of his hands across Sam's neck and he dropped unconscious to the ground. The driver gave Goldie a cynical nod and picked up Sam's revolver before turning to pursue Liz.

Liz swung round the fence, using momentum to turn the corner onto the Calatex path. Her illusion of safety shattered when out of the double doors ahead of her strolled Hendrik Gerber, his lean bearded face brightening with a welcoming smile. She turned and ran back out into the road, only to find that outside the Calatex gate others waited for her too. She came to a halt in the middle of the street and slowly turned full circle, to find herself surrounded. The only way left open to her by Keast's men was the main entrance to the Institute. She ran inside, hoping she might evade her pursuers in the factory offices. They quickly followed her into the building.

The double doors leading to the two passages from reception were both shut and barred against her. She turned at bay against the rarely used doors to the factory floor as Keast's men pressed through the entrance, and shied back from them in fear.

Suddenly the doors gave way behind her. With the roar of the press filling her ears, she fell backwards onto the factory floor. Her pursuers were as startled as she was by her unexpected reprieve. She took advantage of the chance and swiftly ran off into the maze of working machinery. Though her shoes clattered across the hard floor, the rhythmic pounding of the press camouflaged her footsteps. She tried to locate her pursuers psychically as she ran but was distracted by the constant noise around her and had to rely on intuition alone to choose her path. She also looked out for a wall, for only in a wall would she find an exit door.

An alarm bell pealed. Within seconds the press and its ancillary machines shut down. In the ensuing quiet a cry rose up to evacuate the building. Footsteps clattered down the aisles towards the emergency exits. Liz moved along an unused side aisle parallel to the main evacuation route, hoping she might escape in the throng. When she came to a junction, she cautiously looked around the corner, only to find her plan foiled: Rolf Krueger was standing with the foreman at the door to the yard, checking out each employee who passed.

The evacuation was over in seconds. The emergency exits slammed shut and locked. The power turned off and the building fell silent. The mechanical environment of the shop floor took on a foreboding and oppressive air in the dim twilight beaming through the grimy windows in the high roof.

Liz slipped off her court shoes so that she could move about more stealthily. As she tucked the shoes into her handbag, a faint noise from behind made her spin round. Sandy Angus' porcine face leered at her through the gloom, his arms extended to catch her. Before his grip tightened, she screamed and broke away from him to flee back down the aisle. She turned the corner and dived under a production line roller belt, hoping her black dress would conceal her in its shadows. When Sandy Angus turned the corner after her, she had disappeared.

'Easy prey!' Krueger remarked nearby.

'Quiet!' Keast ordered, further away.

Liz pinpointed their positions by ear and scanned the factory psychically, sensing several more people on the shop floor. She heard Sandy Angus moving stealthily closer to her hiding place and hoped he would not notice her, but remembered too late that he was psychic too. He dropped his feint of walking past and dived down to grasp her arm. She swung her handbag at him and struck him across the face with the heels of her shoes. As he sprang back cursing, she crawled through to the other side of the roller belt, leaving it as an obstacle for him while she took flight again.

The lights came back on, catching Liz in the middle of an aisle. She froze, and then looked fearfully round to see who had spotted her out in the open. To her relief the aisle was empty. She scrambled up a ladder onto an inspection platform above the process machinery. From there she tried to get visual confirmation of the numbers and identities of the people looking for her.

A short way along the aisle to her left, Hendrik Gerber

stood looking across the floor to the double doors from reception. Jon Keast walked out of a side aisle to join him: they exchanged comments which made them both laugh. Rolf Krueger stood nearby with Sandy Angus, scanning the floor for their quarry. Keast raised his head to look for Liz above eye level, but before he had turned far enough to catch sight of her, a side door from the offices burst open and Doug Angus and the Greek delegate Phineas Andropoulos entered, dragging in Bethany. Even from across the factory floor Liz could tell Bethany was too terrified to protest at their treatment of her. She wondered in concern what the men had done to reduce her friend to such a state of submission.

'Mrs Graham,' Keast called out, 'I only want to have a friendly chat with you. Why not come out? It won't take long, and afterwards you'll wonder what all the fuss was about.'

The cynical thought passed through her mind that if that was all he had wanted he should have tried the phone. She used her vantage point on the inspection platform to assess the exits from the shop floor. The double doors from reception appeared to be her best option for escape.

She climbed back down the ladder to the factory floor, ready to move through the machinery towards the doors while Angus and Andropoulos escorted Bethany out to whatever transport they had waiting at the loading bay. When they did not pass the end of her aisle, she realised she had miscalculated. She cautiously peered around a corner and saw they had stopped beside Keast.

Hendrik Gerber made a comment and walked off towards the loading bay. On Keast's nod, Andropoulos took a firmer hold of Bethany to let Doug Angus join his brother in the shadows. Krueger reached inside his jacket and crossed to Bethany's side, pulling out a Walther PP pistol. Bethany saw the weapon and struggled violently against Andropoulos. Krueger struck her hard across her left cheek with the back of his hand. Bethany stopped struggling. Liz recoiled with a mixture of indignation and fear. She realised that should she end up in their hands, she could expect no less.

'I shall count to ten, Mrs Graham,' Keast announced: 'If you do not give yourself up by then your friend will die. Do not doubt that.'

Liz had no intention of giving herself up to him while she could still scheme a way to escape. Ferry's Bible quotation flashed through her thoughts. She looked at Keast and wondered whether he really would give the order to shoot Bethany. She sensed that all the men around him would obey.

'As you wish,' Keast stated with finality: 'One.'

She looked at Keast and remembered how Alec had described him the day before: a tyrant amongst the merchants of death whose heavy-handed methods had killed tens and whose merchandise had killed hundreds, perhaps thousands. A man like that would give the order; and a man like that would ensure no untrustworthy witnesses survived to tell the tale.

'Two.'

She recalled her defence of Keast the day before out of chagrin after her argument with Alec, and saw how wrong she had been. She was not pleased to realise that Alec too had been wrong about Keast in believing he had only been attacking her to get at him. Two people had already died because Keast feared her influence, and two more would die soon. Bethany's life was also being threatened. Was the avoidance of a chat with Keast about Alec worth risking her life? Liz prayed fervently that she could escape before they harmed Bethany or she betrayed her husband.

'Three.'

She looked at Bethany held there rigidly by Andropoulos, being forced to watch Krueger with the pistol. She remembered their argument the previous evening with televisual recall. Bethany had threatened to commit suicide. Alec had maintained that she lacked the courage; but had she only lacked the opportunity? In Bethany's eyes Liz sensed a new light now, a desperation which could only have been born of a will to live.

'Four.'

Liz realised that she could not risk Bethany's life at the hands of these evil men: the sanctity of life was far more important than the danger she hoped to avoid. The decision was Bethany's to make whether to face the risk, not hers, whether or not she thought Bethany wanted to die. She would have to set aside her fears about Keast's intentions and walk out to save her friend, trusting her Higher Power to protect her through whatever lay ahead. Yet still she felt reluctant to go.

'Five.'

She wondered what Alec would think when Goldie arrived home to tell him his wife had been forced to disobey his every request, simply through trying to save her friend. A brief fear flashed through her mind that Goldie was not alive to tell Alec what had happened, but she dismissed that as she had already dismissed her fears for her own survival, knowing she would have received different warnings beforehand were that to be the case.

'Six.'

She suddenly realised that at that moment she alone was responsible for the outcome of Bethany's plight. Her friend helplessly depended on her decision. Liz had to accept the event as it was and not hope for the arrival of any saviour to rescue her from Keast's blackmail and Bethany from death.

'Seven.'

Liz slipped her shoes back on and slowly emerged onto the aisle with her arms raised. She saw the men's smug expressions, but was more conscious of her handbag swinging from her left hand and knocking against her forearm. How silly she must appear to such villains, she thought, to be so concerned about her bag that she brought that too when giving herself up to them. Then she realised that she no longer felt frightened. Her decision had been made and Bethany saved: her concern now was to keep all her wits about her for the next round, to ensure that she was ready to take advantage of any opportunity to turn the tables.

'Eight.'

'Okay, I give myself up. You have all the trumps in this hand,' she surrendered.

Keast nodded an instruction to the Angus twins. They came out of the shadows and took hold of Liz's arms to restrain her. Krueger turned the pistol towards her, away from Bethany who fell back in Andropoulos' grip, crying with relief.

'How touching for you, Miss Broome, to find that your best friend did surrender rather than see you die,' Keast said, his manner implying the criticism that Liz would have come out far sooner had she been a true friend.

Only then did Bethany realise what her depressive drunkenness had caused her friend to face.

'Oh, God, Liz: please forgive me,' she pleaded in tears.

'You were forgiven before you asked, Bethany. As Mr Keast knows, I am the idealist. I wouldn't let anyone die to save me from an unpleasant chat, even him. Words aren't cheap, but they're a lot cheaper than death.'

'Really, Mrs Graham? You will find the majority disagrees with you here,' Keast warned, his eyes glinting dangerously.

He projected a deep-rooted malice into her thoughts to undermine her confidence, but she identified his ploy and threw him out of her mind. Where before he had seemed a sinister man she preferred to shun, she now saw him as a ruthless tyrant she was duty-bound to depose. But when she looked into his eyes in defiance of his attempts to control her, once again her body rebelled against her censorship and responded to his potent virility. She averted her gaze and hastily sheathed herself in the blue-white light of divine protection. He realised his failure to undermine her confidence and sought instead to break it, hoping that her foundation of faith was less secure than she supposed.

'Defiance will get you nowhere fast; to the grave faster!' he warned venomously, not breaking his glare.

She tossed her head, impatient with his rhetoric. Sandy

Angus shook her roughly for her impudence, and his brother warned her, 'Don't be a fool: give Jon five minutes alone with you, he'll have all he wants to know. Don't make it inevitable.'

She turned her head to answer Douggie but did not take her eyes off Keast. 'Don't try to fool me with empty promises, Mr Angus. This charade has been well choreographed, so if I am to die that will be too. Though I don't understand why you needed such a performance today, Mr Keast, when you could simply have kept me here yesterday afternoon.'

'You didn't know enough yesterday afternoon,' Keast replied.

His comment opened another door on his cunning to her: she was taken aback to realise that he had deliberately set her up to argue with Alec about him and had manipulated her natural curiosity to ensure she would have all his questions answered.

'Really? So now you've got Pandora's box!' She risked a barter: 'Bethany's played the part you forced on her; she's lured me here to you. Please let her go now.'

'Don't you think her worries are over!' Sandy Angus remarked with a grin.

'Why not? You've got me. Why can't she go?'

'Your friend is my queen of trumps,' Keast said: 'She will not finish playing her part until you finish playing yours.'

Liz saw through his gaze to the edge of darkness inside his mind and recoiled to confront such evil. Whatever his demands, she would have to capitulate to him or Bethany would die. His eyes locked into hers and mocked her with his advantage. He knew her well, far better than she had realised from their first short meeting, and had shown her for what she was to both herself and the men who held her. She nodded to him in acceptance of her defeat.

Keast took the pistol from Krueger and walked over to Liz. Bethany screamed in panic at the thought of what she might be about to witness. Krueger struck her back into silence.

Keast studied Liz's heart-shaped face for a moment. Using

the muzzle of the gun he moved her hair back from her large green eyes and caressed her right cheek. Then the muzzle moved down her neck and lifted her crucifix on its gold chain. He noted that she flinched yet did not protest: though she had a healthy desire to live she was not afraid of death; but she was afraid of the sexual implications of his steel caress.

He handed Krueger's pistol back and instructed the men to take her and Bethany out to their cars waiting at the loading bay. Hendrik Gerber intercepted them at the door with a syringe containing a cocktail of tranquillisers in his right hand. He injected Bethany to prevent further trouble from her, and then approached Liz with a second syringe. Liz struggled desperately against the Angus twins' firm hold to avoid being given the injection, in case the substances it contained had been deliberately chosen to undermine her seven-year abstinence from addictive mood-altering drugs. Gerber mistook her alarm to be fear of a lethal shot.

'It will only put you to sleep for a few hours,' he reassured.

She struggled all the more but failed to break the Angus twins' grip or escape the injection. Sandy and Doug then bundled her roughly into the back seat of Keast's midnight blue Rolls Royce. Keast and Gerber got in on either side of her in the back, while Krueger sat in the front beside the young driver. Ahead of them, the Anguses put Andropoulos and Bethany in the back of their powder blue Jaguar and drove out onto the road to lead the way north.

Outside the factory gates, the evacuation drill had ended and the workers were returning to their posts. The bread van had long since gone. Liz's limousine, and Goldie, had gone too; and the only sign of the articulated lorry's collision with the wall was a gap in the brickwork which was already being repaired. Liz saw the external return to normal as the sedative distanced her from it, and handed her situation over to her Higher Power to resolve, sensing that for the moment she had no hope of help from elsewhere.

She turned her head dazedly to look at Keast, all too aware of his proximity to her, and accidentally caught his eye before he could avert his gaze. His guard was down: once more she felt the intense hatred which burned within him as a constant flame. But this time she did not recoil, for she sensed that the emotions fuelling that fire came from an unhealed bitterness. She could almost touch the emotional damage which had made him block out the consolation of love so completely from his life in his lust to harness hatred's dangerous power. Her compassionate gaze burned into him with the searing force of an acid. He turned swiftly away.

'But who hated you first?' she whispered.

He turned back, unsettled by her words. She had already fallen unconscious. Beyond her, outside the smoked glass windows the busy city streets passed by. Inside the car, Hendrik Gerber watched Keast in concern through the rear-view mirror, while Keast studied Liz and wondered why she of all people was the person to oppose him. The innate peace in her tranquil face had somehow chilled all the joy from his victory.

2 : 12

Liz woke to find herself in a small bare modern office, lying on a bench couch created from three upholstered chairs. Bethany loomed over her like a blurred monolith that reached up into the pulsating white ceiling. Liz wiped her eyes, remembering the unidentified injection given her earlier after the chase at P.S.I. in Chelsea, and decided not to risk trying to sit until she had an idea of how the drug had affected her.

'Didn't they give you as much?' she asked.

Bethany sniggered and sat clumsily on a chair beside her.

'You forget I've had practice recently: recovering from a tranquilliser jab is nothing to two bottles of Nuits St Georges. Wait till the ceiling slows down before you move your legs unless you want to say hello to your lunch again.'

'What lunch? I was calling round to take you out for lunch when they snatched you, so I'm starving. I guess round here condemned men don't get anything to eat or drink. At least you sound a bit happier.'

'Is that what this is: the condemned cell?' Bethany's bizarre lack of concern made her sound more drunk than alarmed.

Liz was too busy trying to stand up to answer. Despite her efforts to control her uncoordinated limbs, her movements were so unsteady that she fell back onto the makeshift couch with her head spinning. She paused for a few moments in a seated position to recover her balance and realised that she felt drunk too.

'You know, Beth, given the choice between here and the dentist, I would probably end up here. I have a very unrealistic fear of the dentist.'

Bethany looked at her in disbelief.

'Liz, I'm sure I didn't imagine that weird scene in that factory, so it must be a lot more serious than the dentist. If that really was real, they'll be coming to question you in a few minutes. We could both be dead in an hour.'

'Don't fret, Beth; we've all got to die sometime. You can take heart that the signs didn't foretell that for us two today. No, the two people who still have to die are Rolf Krueger and Doug Angus.'

Bethany was not sure how to receive such a matter-of-fact prophesy of doom.

'Not that dishy German? What a waste!'

Liz gave her a double look, unsure whether she had heard her correctly.

'You're not telling me you fancied him, after he threatened you at gunpoint and kept hitting you to shut you up?'

'Well, you're a fine one to talk, the way you looked at Jonathan Keast.'

'What d'you mean?'

'Oh, come on! The last time I saw you looking like that was the first time you met Guy Simms at Uncle Harry's bookshop. Put your tongue back in your mouth!'

Liz paled to discover her attraction had been so easily identified.

'But Bethany, I'm happily married to Alec. It's such a betrayal!'

'Nonsense! The only betrayal would be in what you might do about it. Just because I find Rolf Krueger sexy doesn't mean I'll jump in the sack with him. A warm fur coat's sexy too, but you won't find me hugging a man-eating tiger.'

Liz looked at her friend and wondered why they were talking nonsense in such a predicament.

'Beth, you've got to help me sober up before the questions start, or get me out of here. Do you have any idea where we are?'

'When I looked out the window, the street seemed vaguely familiar; but I'm not used to looking at London from the fourth floor so I couldn't be sure. The sign on the alley opposite says Gower Yard, W1.'

The name sounded familiar to Liz. She lurched unsteadily across the room and clung to the windowsill for support to look out. On the far side of the busy one-way street she recognised an electronics shop Alec had visited several times, twice while she was shopping with him up town.

'Tottenham Court Road. So this must be Neptune House, the headquarters of P.S.I. I must let Goldie know.'

'Of course! Ask them to unlock the door and bring a phone! What does it matter where we are, Liz? It's the parlour games we have to worry about.'

Liz shut her ears to Bethany's voice and concentrated on locating Goldie's psychic image. After she felt she had tuned in to her, she tried to transmit her whereabouts telepathically with a request for help. She stopped almost immediately when a key turned in the door.

Hendrik Gerber strolled in with a jaunty step and a friendly greeting. Bethany ignored his enquiry into their health and demanded to know the time. Liz glanced at her left wrist to answer but discovered her watch had gone. She gripped the windowsill for support and looked for her handbag but that had gone too.

'It is time for Mrs Graham's interview,' Gerber announced.

He offered Liz his arm, knowing the sedative he had used would still be disorientating her. She accepted his support and realised with dismay just how much she needed it in the larger space of the corridor outside. She wondered whether her mental ability was equally impaired and longed for a mug of strong coffee to flush the drug out of her system.

Gerber took her to another small furnished office, equipped with two office chairs either side of a black vinyl-topped desk. He helped her sit in the chair in front of the desk and adjusted the armrests to support her. Then he leaned back against the desktop with his arms folded as though he were waiting for something. Liz tried to use the waiting time to send another message to Goldie. Before she had located her again, Gerber looked her in the face and shook his head with a reproving smile.

'Do you think we cannot hear you, Mrs Graham? There are techniques for all these skills, and ways to block them. You may be talented, but you are an amateur here among professionals, and the drug I gave you will affect that too.'

'What was in the shot?' Liz ventured apprehensively.

Gerber looked at her more thoughtfully. 'Nothing from the cocktails you used to take: I had to make sure it worked.'

His answer left her both relieved to know she had not broken her vow of abstinence, and uncomfortable to realise that he too knew more about her than she would have liked. She was about to comment when a knock at the door made her hesitate.

Gerber opened the door to admit Terry Carter and then left the office, his duty done. Terry placed a coffee tray on the desk and sat down opposite Liz. She poured out two cups of strong dark coffee from the tall white china pot while Liz watched, pleasantly surprised to have been proved wrong.

'You don't take sugar, do you; just a dash of milk,' Terry said, handing her a brimming cup.

'What's it spiked with?' Liz joked with barbed intent.

'There's nothing in it that shouldn't be, I promise: just water and coffee and milk,' Terry replied, her voice pitched slightly higher than normal. 'You're here for the little chat Jon promised. If you start being more sensible about all this you really do have nothing to fear. Jon even said you should talk with me rather than one of the men as we already know each other from outside, so to speak.'

Terry sipped her coffee. Liz took a cautious sip from her cup and found the bitter drink cleansed her palate and sharpened her senses. She drank the rest thirstily and set down her empty cup with a nod of appreciation. Terry promptly poured her a refill. As she set the coffeepot back down Liz saw the watch on her left wrist read a quarter to seven. Liz smiled again more confidently, having thwarted her captors' negligent attempts to disorientate her in place and time, and sat in patient silence, unsettling Terry who had expected defensive protests from her.

'Aren't you going to ask me what our chat's about?'

Liz considered this.

'Why should I? You'll tell me soon enough.'

Terry sipped her coffee to hide her own uncertainty in the face of Liz's passive resistance. She opened a drawer and took out some leaflets which she handed to her. Liz glanced through the leaflets which were about the benefits of joining P.S.I. She looked at the pictures but read little of the text as her concentration was still poor. After what seemed like an appropriate length of time, she handed the leaflets back and drained her second cup of coffee. Terry poured her another refill.

'Well, what do you think?'

'Don't tell me, after all that's happened, you want me to join!'

'Of course we want you to join. You're a very gifted psychic, much more than you think; and in the right hands you could go far. I knew as soon as I met you; and as Jon's secretary, naturally I told him about you. He was most insistent I should ask you to join us: where else would you find the special training you need, he said, than here with us at P.S.I., the society which works for the very causes you hold dear. That's why you're here today.'

Liz stared at Terry in unspoken astonishment, wondering whether she had been told anything of the events that lunchtime. Then she remembered Terry had been waiting for her outside Briarbank the night before after tricking Bethany into luring her into danger. Liz decided not to comment further until this dangerous woman had finished her presentation. She sipped her coffee and nodded to her to continue.

'Maybe I should tell you a bit about P.S.I., Liz, in case the rumours you've heard about us have been wrong. P.S.I. is a modern go-ahead society with a corporate constitution, and its logo is Neptune's trident, the Greek letter psi. It was founded twenty years ago to unite, educate and inform psychic people and others who want to advance psychic causes. The society is established in fourteen countries in Europe and the Middle East, with our headquarters here in London where we co-ordinate the organisation, information and campaigns. We also provide a dedicated printing service. Members include top politicians and civil servants, leading industrialists and merchants, famous clairvoyants, spiritualists and healers, and many others who join to support our cause or to develop their talents to their fullest extent. And that is why we'd like you to join too, because we recognise your special talents and know that with the right training you could become one of our most valued members. Tomorrow morning, P.S.I. starts its twentieth annual conference, our forum for debate where we draw up our policy for the coming year. And you can attend too, if you say yes.'

Liz felt uplifted by Terry's flattery and mentally stepped back, knowing not to risk being weakened by her pride.

'Aye, but there'll be strings attached to that, I'm sure! What am I to say yes to?'

Terry answered her question even though she sensed she had no intention of complying.

'You would say yes to joining P.S.I. and learning more about our work, to allowing us to erase today from your memory and assess the full extent of your talents so that we can develop your potential.'

Liz considered the list, but viewed the image from a different angle and saw only the misuse of drugs and interrogation. Agreeing to that would leave her helpless to prevent herself betraying Alec's confidences to Keast, who would not be slow to use them against his adversary. Liz could not agree to anything which might endanger Alec, no matter what he had ordered her to do for her own safety: her love for him compelled her to play the hero. She gave Terry a resolute smile and began to answer her propaganda.

'You say that P.S.I. is a club for psychic people to pursue psychic causes. That isn't what killed Andrew Ferry, or Joe Watson, or Pierre Eve, or those members in Beirut. There is no psychic issue behind the incident today at the P.S.I. printing house - you don't know how the driver of the artic came off, do you, or what happened to my mother-in-law after Sam and Theo were downed? No, Terry, it's more than rumours that make me think twice: what you describe doesn't match what I've found. All I see here is a group of mindless people ruled like puppets by Keast and his happy dust. There's no more behind the polished veneer.'

'Don't you see? That's why you're needed,' Terry whispered urgently, but Liz mistrusted her intentions and ignored her interruption.

'Keast is not the only leading member I don't trust: all the others I've met give me grave doubts too. The Angus twins are hardly a benevolent couple, and Krueger and Gerber are positively evil. And then there's Andropoulos, and Marner, whatever happened to him. And my doubts increase every minute about you.'

Liz paused to reorder the thoughts in her woolly mind, giving Terry an opportunity to respond.

'If I may answer your questions, Liz; Inspector Marner will be transferred to another post after your husband's intervention; Mrs King and your bodyguards will shortly wake up in a Surrey beauty spot and find your car has run out of petrol; and the man in the lorry escaped without injury, as did everyone else, after a security guard cracked and went berserk at the press, which was evacuated for safety until his colleagues managed to restrain him - he is now being treated in hospital.'

'Well, remembered, Terry; but do you think that story makes it any better for me? How can I say yes? I know the minds behind the lies: how can I trust the promises of such dangerous men after seeing how far the truth is bent here.'

'But Liz, if you don't say yes, you won't leave here alive.'

The choked edge in Terry's voice told Liz she believed what she said and warned her of other deeper emotions.

'I will not compromise my principles for murderers and drug pedlars!'

An electronic bleep interrupted their confrontation. Terry took a small pager out of her pocket and pressed a button to read the message. Liz used the pause to pour herself another cup of coffee and hand her situation over to the care of her Higher Power. Terry slipped the pager away and turned back with pity in her eyes.

'I'm sorry, Liz. I wanted to spare you this, but you wouldn't let us do it any other way. Mr Keast wishes to see you now.'

She called Gerber back into the office to escort the captive. Liz finished her coffee and stood up with the confidence of faith, ready to face the showdown.

2 : 13

Jonathan Keast stood waiting for his captive at the window of the small office he had chosen for their third meeting. The question Liz had asked him in his car still echoed in his mind, tempting him to indulge in the weakness of self-pity. He resolutely set aside his emotional response to her offered sympathy, for a greater resolve to undermine her faith and through her his adversary Alec Graham.

He could not risk killing Liz for fear of tipping the fine balance of the hostilities with Dr Graham into an out-and-out war which he could only lose: from past experience he knew his adversary could turn insanely vengeful. How long he could safely keep Liz he was not sure, but he intended to turn her into a far more useful negotiating card before her husband arrived to rescue her.

The sodium amytal in the coffee Liz had drunk meant that he did not need to confront her: the drug would soon do its work. Despite this, he chose to do so because he desired to master her, body, soul and spirit. He knew that her capitulation at the press had been only partial and he wanted nothing less than total control.

Gerber brought Liz in and locked the door behind him after he left. She stood patiently at the edge of the room, waiting for Keast to turn away from the window and look at her. He appeared deep in thought but was operating on a different plane, psychically assessing her strengths and weaknesses while the residual effects of the first drug made her negligent to protect her psychic image. He found four strands of emotion in her: the calm from her faith masking her fear of committing a betrayal and her guilt over her attraction to him.

'Sit down, Mrs Graham,' he ordered without turning back.

She complied without comment and sat on one of two hard

seats in front of the desk. His manner warned her to expect a long session. She sensed he was deliberately cultivating his hatred of her in retaliation for her having unsettled him. She also knew he was trying to increase her apprehension by making her wait, and worked to ignore it.

When he realised his silence was having no effect, he changed tactics and sat down on the edge of the desk only inches from her. He looked down on her as though she were a foolish teenager.

'So you are Dr Graham's painted doll.'

He grasped her chin with his right hand and forced her head to either side to inspect her damaged makeup. Then he held her face firmly to force her to look at him.

'It didn't take long for your paint to crack.'

She tried to pull away from him to avoid looking into the burning hatred of his eyes but could not break his grip.

'I have been studying you for some time, Mrs Graham, and I have come to some interesting conclusions which you will no doubt deny.'

His grip tightened and his tone hardened.

'You seem to think you are above everything, like some goddess; you think everyone is at your beck and call: you believe your opinions are so valued that you need only express disapproval and the things you dislike disappear. There is something you have got to learn, madam. You have left your faery castle behind here for the real world: it's not that way now!'

He tossed her head aside and stood up to pace the floor while he harangued her. She hung her head, resolving to use silence as her defence.

'I've had enough of your childish insults, your unfounded suppositions, your prejudiced decisions. I have no more patience to humour you. You will learn that my name is not one to be mentioned lightly. And when I speak you will listen to me, girl!'

He lashed out at her face and struck her left cheek with the back of his left hand, the ring on his middle finger drawing blood. The unexpected blow stunned her momentarily out of her concentration upon a mark on the desktop which she had been studying to prevent his verbal attack from causing damage. After a pause she shook her head to throw off the shock. For a brief second her eyes narrowed at him before she returned her attention to the score mark on the desktop. He saw her first fleeting hint of resentment and knew that her defences were weakening. To confuse her, he changed tactics again and sat down opposite her on the far side of the desk.

'You realise of course that we are completely alone here. I can do whatever I want to you, and no-one will interfere. And I have many means to persuade you to obedience. Would you not be more sensible to agree to my demands now rather than let your pride destroy you - must you prove the truth of your brag not to compromise for murderers and drug pedlars? Say yes now, and you will be free to go as soon as you have fulfilled my conditions.'

She hardly heard his words for working out that the desktop score had been gouged out with a metal ruler. When she still did not respond, he realised the device she was using to parry his attack and changed tactics again. He moved back round the desk to sit closer to her.

'Say yes to me now, or you will find the number of my conditions grows the longer we play these games,' he warned, and reached over to caress her neck.

She struck out at his arm in automatic defence. He easily caught her wrist to deflect the blow and forced her arm back. She sprang up to pull away from him, knocking aside her chair. He deftly caught her other wrist and jerked her towards him as he stood up over her. She struggled helplessly against his vice-like grip. Her obvious fear of the possible consequences fanned his desire to subjugate her all the more. He pressed his mouth against her lips, easily overpowering her attempts to resist.

Suddenly he threw her off onto the floor as though she had

burnt him. He hastily resumed his seat on the far side of the desk, placing a physical barrier between them to mirror the emotional barrier he had just discovered for his own safety he must erect.

Liz got up from the floor and sat back on the chair, her body trembling. His possible intentions alarmed her, but because she was reacting on the emotional plane of fear and betrayal, she could no longer penetrate his screened thoughts to discover what those intentions were. She sat on guard, ready at any moment to spring back from his further advances.

Keast saw her defensive posture and began his next, safer gambit. After phoning an instruction to an internal number, he raised his head and studied Liz with arrogant eyes.

'So we are back with Bethany. You foolish child! Why do you force my hand when I have all the aces?'

'The hand is not necessarily the game; and I am no gambler.'

He smiled at her failure to sustain her silence against him so soon and quickly coaxed her to talk again before she appreciated the significance of her slip.

'You gambled yesterday, when you called at P.S.I. Chelsea.'

'Yes, I suppose it was. But you gambled then too.'

'Certainly; but I do not deny being a gambler. You even went against the advice of your bodyguard to pay that visit.'

'It seemed no gamble at the time.'

The door opened and Hendrik Gerber entered with Bethany. Rolf Krueger followed them in and locked the door after them. Bethany and Liz looked at each other in apprehensive recognition. Krueger placed a black case on the desk and opened it. He took out the Walther PP pistol, loaded a magazine into its butt, screwed a silencer onto its muzzle, pulled the slide back and released it to load the first round.

Liz shifted her gaze uneasily between the gun and Keast. He was watching her with an impassive expression which told her just how large a gamble she had taken. His eyes commanded her to give in to him. She recalled his enforced embrace and shook her head.

'You must be joking.'

'Shoot her,' Keast ordered.

Krueger swiftly turned the pistol on Bethany. She screamed.

'Wait!' Liz shouted.

The pistol stopped, unfired. Keast glowered at Liz with an unspoken command to speak. She stalled for time with a tirade of bluff.

'Before we continue this farce, Mister Keast, may I remind you that you have not yet asked any questions for me to answer. You've just forced me to take part in a pantomime which starred you, was supported by you, was written, directed and produced by you; and what for? I can only presume to impress us with your magnificent armoury. Fine, we are impressed. Bethany is terrified, of a man who does not live up to his reputation; and I am still sitting here waiting, for a man who contradicts himself with his every statement instead of getting to the point. Stop playing these foolish games with us while you're still ahead. Let us both walk out of here now still unharmed, and I promise you will hear no more about it.'

Even as she railed against him, her patronising manner told Keast he had won their battle of wills. She saw his confidence at that moment when all was held in the balance, and realised too late that her unchristian arrogance showed how much her faith had slipped. He went straight in with a full attack before she had the chance to fall back on prayer and repair the breach.

'You want questions, Mrs Graham? Try these. What do you know? What is your husband doing? Who has helped you? What are your plans? Where do your two guests fit in? What connections do you have with our former French delegate, the late Pierre Eve? And which way have you chosen to take? Will you continue to pretend you are sitting on the fence, or will you take one of the sides? Or are you going to become a third side?'

He paused to give her the chance to answer but knew his sudden aggressive questioning had stunned her into speechlessness, his tactical reply to her request to see him as he really was, showing her just how much she had gambled.

'Come on, answer me! Or do you want more? Why are you trying to depose the leadership of P.S.I.? What do you hope to achieve by fighting me? How will you save yourself, now that the tables have turned and you are on your own? What will you do when the words run out and the only thing between you and death is me?'

She reeled under the blow of his last question. Helpless to rally her previous composure, she lapsed into the self-pity of a younger age.

'Oh God! Leave me alone. I can't take any more of your bullying, or your threats, or your bloody guns. Please, give me a break; just a couple of minutes alone.'

'I will certainly not give you a break: you represent the material enemy P.S.I. must fight in this war of spiritual forces. So tell me, what do you know about P.S.I.'

She begged him to leave her alone but he refused, impervious to her tears, hungry for her capitulation. He repeated his question more harshly. She curled up with her arms over her head to shut out his voice. Gerber forced her to unbend, holding her by her shoulders so that she could not stop herself hearing Keast and had to look at him whenever she opened her eyes. Again Keast demanded an answer to his question. Her hesitant stutter of a response was not enough.

'Look at the gun,' he commanded.

Her eyes moved sidelong to stare at Krueger whose left hand controlled petrified Bethany in the chair beside her while he held the pistol in his right. She watched with mounting horror as the muzzle of the gun moved slowly across from Bethany until it pointed straight at her.

'Don't shoot! Please, leave me a moment, to collect my thoughts.'

Keast nodded and took the gun from Krueger, holding the weapon with pleasure at the power it bestowed on its worshippers. For a moment he admired its gleaming form, lightly stroking its smooth steel and balancing its weight in his hands. Then he checked that the hammer was cocked and aimed the gun at Liz.

'You've had enough time to collect everybody's thoughts.'

Bethany sprang up and dived across the desk to snatch the gun from Keast's hands, her sudden move catching him out. Krueger struck out to stop her as the gun went off, and the shot deflected towards the wall. Bethany screamed and fell to the floor stunned. Liz thought in horror that her friend had been shot and tried to go to her, but Gerber forcibly held her back in her seat. Krueger picked up the gun from the floor and returned it to Keast who nodded a command to him. He dragged Bethany's limp body out of the room. After they had gone Keast turned the pistol straight back on Liz.

'We've reached the last act of this pantomime, Mrs Graham,' he said. 'Look into my eyes.'

She shifted her gaze to look at his eyes but strove not to look into them in case she saw through them once again to the darkness of his inner being. That was not enough for him. He locked and cocked the hammer of the pistol to reinforce his order.

'Look into my eyes,' he insisted.

She obeyed; though it made her sick with fear. To gaze into the depths of his dark eyes made her feel she was falling into a bottomless pit filled with indefinable terrors, as though he were taking her away from physical existence and returning her to a spiritual realm between universes where unloving souls roam lost in a hopeless search for peace.

'Relax,' he said.

She cried out in fear that she could not, but despite herself she felt her limbs relinquishing their tension. Her eyelids became heavy and her head dropped. Somewhere in the recesses of her mind a voice warned her she had been drugged again and urged her to fight against it, but the desire to sleep was becoming too great to resist. One by one her muscles relaxed throughout her body. Gerber supported her rather than restrained her.

'Relax,' Keast repeated more gently.

Distantly she noticed he had locked the pistol again and set it aside. Without its threat she felt lost in a conflict of loyalties. Though she knew she should use the advantage to take flight, her body was completely unresponsive to her will. She could no longer resist the persuasiveness of his commanding yet beguiling voice.

'You have nothing to fear now: nothing will harm you,' he reassured. 'I am going to take you away on a journey, a journey into the past...'

'Into the past,' she repeated; and mists swirled round her consciousness until all became dark.

2 : 14

Liz woke to the call that breakfast had arrived. She sat up on her couch of office chairs, astonished to hear Bethany's voice. Bethany smiled at her from her seat at a desk where she was lifting plate-lids to see what had been provided.

'Welcome back to the condemned cell, Liz: two full English breakfasts and the biggest pot of coffee I've ever seen. You must have put in a good word with the management last night.'

'But you're alive, Bethany! I'm sure I saw you shot dead. Or was that just a dream?'

Liz strove to recall the events of the previous day but found them veiled in a mist. All she could firmly remember was her failure to resist Keast's hypnotism.

'Oh, God! Forgive me my lapse of faith, that let such an evil man better me,' she cried in regret.

'Shut up and eat your breakfast,' Bethany ordered without sympathy between mouthfuls, having been warned that others could hear their conversation: 'Save the regrets department till later: you never know when they may take the food away again. They're a funny lot here.'

Liz obediently sat down at the desk and ate, suddenly aware of how hungry and thirsty she felt. She tried to remember when she had last eaten but found her recall of events the previous day elusive.

'Oh, my memory! Keast must have tried to erase it.'

'It's a side effect of a drug they gave us: Terry told me so when she dropped off this food. That's why we're both still here now enjoying breakfast, so stop fishing, shut up and get eating.'

Liz realised Bethany must be warning her to be guarded for a reason and abandoned questioning her to try a different way of refreshing her memory. She used a device she had first developed in family conflicts to check whether her mother was telling the truth. As she ate, she identified the last event she could clearly recall, the last time she and Alec had made love, and let her subconscious replay that and subsequent events as images on a television screen in the background of her conscious thoughts. The scenes were distorted and incomplete but enough to help her understand her present context. At length she found only Keast's final interrogation was totally missing. She felt a flash of concern about what had happened while she was so completely in his power; but hastily banished such weakening fears from her thoughts. Escape was more pressing: she sent Goldie the telepathic message *Neptune House* with the image of a trident.

Bethany had finished eating. She poured them both more coffee.

'The traffic noise is dropping outside: it must be well after nine,' she commented. 'The conference starts at ten. Members only, of course: we shall be well away from the main event, in the club's T.V. lounge upstairs.'

175

'Really? Miss Carter must have given you a lecture with breakfast.'

Bethany smiled enigmatically and stared into her coffee cup with the distant interest she had so often paid wine glasses recently.

'And so to the regrets department,' she opened hesitantly. After a pause she continued, 'Although their drug's made me forget what happened yesterday, it hasn't wiped away the decision I reached.'

She paused again, finding her confession hard even though she realised there was little she could say that Liz did not already know. Liz watched her sympathetically but would not pry into her thoughts without invitation.

'I keep thinking of Sunday night, Liz, when I turned on you because of that fake photo. Yet you were the only one who really understood! You never asked what a woman like me was doing with a no-good like Mike, the way everyone else did: they couldn't grasp how much I love him, whatever he may be. Only you saw that, even though you didn't like him; and when he left me you were the only one who tried to mend the hurt I felt. Only you stopped me from gassing myself; but I did need anaesthesia so I drowned it in drink, while you tried to show me there are still some things to live for. But I didn't believe you, not until yesterday....'

She sipped her coffee, trying to remember the incident that had been her turning point. The whole of the day seemed just a blur.

'Something happened yesterday to open my eyes: suddenly I can see all the good things in life again, all the things I don't want to leave, at least not without a last goodbye: simple things like sunshine and flowers, crowded streets and lunch at the restaurant on the common - silly little things I'd never given a thought to before. Something happened that gave me back my will to live, and I have you to thank for that, Liz. I've had plenty of time to think since then, and though it's all pretty confused,

I've been trying to work out where I went wrong. I've been a stupid fool; but I am learning from it, and I swear I'll never go so low again, over anything.'

Liz gave her friend a hug.

'That's wonderful news, Beth: it makes all we've been through worthwhile.'

'But why should you have to go through so much too, when you gained nothing?'

'Ah, but I have. I never really understood until now, how the power of evil is also a power greater than myself, which a person could choose to found their life upon much as I have chosen the power of God. But the Devil destroys in the process: he tricks men like Keast into suppressing the power of love until it turns to hatred. It's always been my duty to warn those riding to destruction to turn back; but it's also my duty to help them if they want to save themselves; and that is why I'm here. I had written P.S.I. off; but I was wrong to judge: it's not too late for P.S.I. to change direction. And I have a part to play here; but not in my own power: no, only if I rely solely upon the power of God.'

Bethany looked blankly at her friend, her spiritual flights totally beyond her capacity to comprehend. She remarked, 'Liz, your toast has gone cold: all the butter has melted and set.'

Liz smiled at her gentle rebuke. 'Quite right, Beth: I should leave that sort of talk for Sundays.' She was about to speak further when the door opened.

The Angus twins walked in. They had dressed in suits for the conference and their porcine eyes sparkled with high spirits, but their good mood could not mask from Liz the shadow of evil around one and the growing shadow of death around the other.

'Good morning, ladies, and welcome to the ranks of P.S.I.' Sandy greeted. 'Here are your membership cards. When you're ready, we'll take you to your places in the C.C.T.V. lounge for the conference.'

Bethany took her membership card and slipped it into her

pocket without a thought. Liz inspected her card closely and noted her signature inside it was dated the Sunday just gone.

'This is a forgery. I didn't sign this on Sunday.'

'You signed it last night,' Doug stated in a manner which warned her not to make it an issue.

She looked thoughtfully at the card and realised the subtle motive behind it. Her condoning signature would significantly weaken any accusation she might make against the society about its treatment of her.

'I understand,' she conceded, and touched Doug's left forearm to gain his full attention.

'Douglas Angus, be warned yourself: if you don't change course at once, it will be to your significant cost.'

'Not that one again!' Sandy scoffed: 'She's already tried it on Rolf!'

Doug nodded, but he was far less amused by her warning than his brother was. He hastily propelled Bethany out of the office so that Liz would not see his expression of dismay.

Sandy escorted Liz, following them more slowly as he chatted sociably about the conference and how much he looked forward to working with her in the society. Liz gave him non-committal replies, realising he was not aware she had remembered enough to see the society for what it still was rather than the public image Keast was now trying to make her think it had.

The Angus twins took Liz and Bethany along to a windowless but comfortable lounge on the same floor, where a dozen armchairs stood grouped around a television screen. They introduced them to the two members who had been entrusted to look after them there: Pete Corrie, an under-manager in his mid-forties over for the day from P.S.I. Chelsea; and Tim Jackson, a strongly psychic young man in a sweatshirt and jeans, with a familiar spirit guide whose presence set Liz on edge. The Angus twins then left to return to their conference duties elsewhere.

Pete welcomed Liz and Bethany with more coffee poured

from a fresh pot on a table at the back of the room, while Tim tuned in the television set. Bethany took a cup and sat down in an armchair, to find her shoulder-bag lying nearby as though she had left it there earlier. Liz turned and noticed her handbag by another chair. She gratefully picked it up and sat down to check its contents, retrieving her cosmetics so that she could make up her face.

Pete dropped into the armchair next to Liz, his gaze resting uncertainly on Tim.

'We've all been looking forward to meeting you so much, Mrs Graham,' he breathed. 'Especially after all the trouble you've put us to. You have a sharp sense of humour.'

'I do; but did you get all the jokes? I found some of the humour here a little heavy,' she replied tactically.

She scanned his psychic image as she applied her lipstick and relaxed at what she saw.

'What an appropriate name you have, Peter the rock, and how new you are. What are you doing here?'

'This is where I was told to come.' His inflection conveyed he had followed the order of a higher power than the hierarchy of P.S.I.

She nodded in understanding and followed his apprehensive gaze to Tim who was still tuning in the television. The familiar spirit co-inhabiting Tim objected to her attention and tried to intimidate her by planting malevolence in her mind. She signed herself with the rosy cross and chased it out of her thoughts. The unsettled familiar protested by troubling Tim's dexterity. Bethany saw the young man becoming increasingly clumsy but could not understand why, when all Liz seemed to be doing was watching him with a benign smile.

'Is that another example of Keast's work?' Liz asked Pete, inclining her head towards Tim as the television screen cleared.

Her simple question completely upturned Pete's appreciation of what had been happening in P.S.I. Until that moment he had always understood the evidence he had found at work to incriminate the Angus twins rather that Keast in the supply of less than legal drugs to members like Tim. The new perspective placed all the facts he had failed to understand at the time into an all too convincing picture which chilled him with dismay.

'Yes, that is,' he admitted.

'Then why didn't you stop it long ago, if you saw?'

Her question caught Tim's veiled attention.

Pete turned away, ashamed to admit to this brave young woman that he had been too frightened of the consequences to betray men like the Angus twins. Then, he had had no alternative: now, in her at last he did.

'I must warn the others,' he resolved, standing.

'You'll do nothing of the sort,' Tim ordered, straightening up.

'What d'you get out of it - free scag?' Bethany spat.

Her non-believing contempt enraged the spirit-controlled young man. He sprang menacingly towards her, making her cower back in her seat.

Pete and Liz leapt across to intervene. The demon threw Tim forward at Liz, spewing a torrent of abuse at her in an unnatural voice. Pete tried to put himself between them, but Liz side-stepped him to place her hand on Tim's shoulder. Tim shrank back as though her touch had burnt him. He tried to shrug her off but could not loosen her hold. The swearing subsided and he sank down in an armchair, cowed and defensive. Liz sat beside him and took hold of his hands.

'Tim, I know you're in there, praying for escape. I have been there too, though with a different drug. You can send the demon packing, as I did; but if you don't change your ways, the demon will come back and bring seven friends with him; as I once found. You cannot save yourself from demons while you sacrifice your life to crack.'

'You were never like this, you fucking rich bint!' Tim spat, and spewed more abuse as the spirit still fought for control.

'Tim!' Pete rebuked. Liz waved at him to stop.

She threw a psychic net around the spirit to quieten it for a while. Then she prayed for a warm red light of healing to come over the troubled, shaking young man. As his tremors calmed, she spoke on.

'When I was fifteen, I didn't understand my psychic abilities: I'd been taught that that sort of thing was just women's intuition, not to be trusted. I used to get these dreams, where I'd see someone dying; then soon after they did die, and I thought I'd put a curse on them. You see, I'd no-one around to talk to who could explain what was happening. And sometimes I went dizzy, and then bad things would happen to me or people around me; and I began to think I was cursed. The only way I could make sense of it all was to believe my life here was a punishment for some heinous crime I'd committed on some other world in some past life; and the only way I thought I could escape my punishment was to die.'

Liz paused, aware that Pete and Bethany had both moved closer to listen. Tim watched her, engrossed, his struggles for the moment forgotten. She sipped her coffee and continued to speak.

'After about the third suicide attempt, I ended up in hospital, on a complicated cocktail of mood affecting drugs which included anti-depressants, sleeping tablets and tranquillisers. Unwittingly the doctors gave me permission to live my life in a drugged stupor: they didn't keep a check on the amount they prescribed, and I was soon taking triple the dose. After a while they said I was better and stopped the drugs. I went through the withdrawals, which they said I couldn't possibly have with these drugs. And back came all those awful dreams. I couldn't cope so I started drinking heavily, and then I tried to kill myself again, and I ended back on the drugs. The doctors told my parents, this is the way your daughter will be for the rest of her life. And my mother cursed me for damaging her career.

'But it got even worse. The doctors had not told me not to drink alcohol when I was taking their drugs, so I did. And one night while I was sitting reading my Tarot cards by candlelight, I heard demons at the window, tapping their long fingernails on the glass to attract my attention. I looked up and saw their ugly pointed faces. "She's ours!" they cried, and I knew they'd come for me. The next eighteen months of my life became a complete blank.

'I now know what happened during that time only because I wrote a diary of sorts: it makes horrible reading. I moved out from my parents' house into a dingy bed-sitter, I mixed with the worst company, and treated my body and my mind with contempt. Many's the time I woke up in a strange place not knowing how I got there. But that's how I found the road to getting better, because one morning I woke up in the doorway of the Antiquarian Bookshop and met a man who'd been through something similar with the drink, a guy Bethany and I know as Uncle Harry. He'd seen me around the village so he knew what I was like. "Isn't it time you did something about yourself?" he asked me. And I found myself telling him all about my life, and my dreams and premonitions; and he didn't laugh. He got me to meet a priest called Father Jay who told me what my dreams and premonitions really meant. But more than that, they convinced me that I could get better, and that it was worth getting better: they gave me hope. Just as they said to me, I say to you, Tim: you can get better, too, if you really want to.'

His shoulders were shaking. Hot tears slid down his cheeks.

'God knows I've tried; but something keeps stopping me. They say all you need is will power, but it just doesn't work that way.'

'Leave the will power to people who don't understand these things. If you really want to get better, give me the little red tin and tell your familiar to go.'

'But how will I cope?' he cried, panicking at the thought of a black future with no help or support to see him through.

'Take that step of faith, Tim, and you will cope, just as I found I could cope. Father Jay can give you the keys to a new way of life just as he gave them to me seven years ago; and I have never looked back. No more drugs, no more drink, no more demons: the freedom to be yourself without fear. That can be yours too: all you have to do to start is give me the tin and tell your familiar to go.'

Slowly Tim's shaking hand went to his shirt pocket. He drew out a small round tin with a red pattern edged in blue. For a moment indecision caught him and the hand froze in mid-air, clutching the tin. Liz opened her right hand beneath his fingers. He released the tin. It fell into her palm.

'Well done: I knew you could do it. Now the familiar.'

She released the bonds which had silenced the spirit, and for a moment it took Tim back over, contorting his face with malevolence and forcing a stream of foul language through his lips. But Tim had already made his decision: in a strangled voice he ordered the spirit to go. It departed with a vengeance, throwing him into a fit and leaving him like an empty husk on the carpeted floor.

Bethany helped Liz lift Tim into a seat. Liz patted his cheeks to bring him round. His tired eyes flickered open. Pete handed him a cup of coffee with an encouraging smile. He took a sip and vacantly gazed round at a world he had not seen properly for three years.

'Tim, you've done a wonderful thing today,' Liz said once he was able to comprehend her. She handed him a card from her handbag. 'If you want to continue on this road, phone this man at once: Father Jay. I know he can help you make it like he helped me: just tell him Lisbeth told you to call. But you must do it right away: you need spiritual protection as well as physical and emotional help.'

Tim looked up at Pete for permission, wanting to go but knowing they were both under orders to guard the two women. Pete knew the risks they would take if Tim went but was inspired by Liz's example to agree.

'Send Charles Lafayette in to cover for you; then go and make that call, Tim. I'm sure the ladies won't cause us any problems while you're sorting yourself out.'

Tim thanked them and hurried out of the lounge. Pete watched him leave and turned back to Liz.

'I thought that sort of thing stopped happening centuries ago!'

'*And greater things than these will you do.* Don't underestimate God, Pete: pray for faith to claim them.'

2 : 15

Shortly before 10 o'clock, Bethany noticed the picture had changed on the lounge C.C.T.V. screen. Down in the modern conference theatre, fourteen delegates had filed in through doors by the semi-circular stage and taken their places round the horseshoe table at the base of the crowded tiers of seats. The volume being cabled to the television increased. Liz and Pete turned to watch.

Jonathan Keast entered the auditorium with Terry at his side. He looked confident and assured as they took their places at the table at the centre of the stage; but Liz sensed that beneath his image he was on edge. The delegates surrounding him were also uneasy behind their facades. They were all key players in his illegal empire, placed in positions of authority so that they could support his network across Europe from the Fertile Crescent to the Atlantic coast; and like him they knew something was wrong.

The audience settled and Keast stood to open the twentieth annual conference of P.S.I. with a short address from the rostrum. While Bethany and Liz watched his polished performance, the lounge door opened and Charles Lafayette slipped in. Pete moved to the back of the room to hold a whispered conversation with him about the events there. As the conference moved on to the first of the delegates' reports, they agreed a course of action and Pete left the lounge.

Charles took his place in the armchair beside Liz; a tall, lean mild-mannered man in his early fifties. When Liz heard the door close, she turned and was startled to see a stranger sitting next to her instead of Pete. He gave her a gentle reassuring smile.

'Tim is making his phone call, and Pete has gone to speak to the other members,' he said, his voice charming with the lilt of a French accent.

'What's been decided?' Liz asked.

'That is for the members to say. Pete is calling a fringe debate on P.S.I. Britain's floor to tell the members what happened here, while the delegates talk in the basement theatre. Were we all blind? Yet we are the psychic experts: my job is to develop psychic talent.'

'Jon Keast is an expert too: only a handful of you will be skilled enough for him to have to guard himself psychically; and most of those he's got onto his side so that he can shift any blame onto them.'

'Like the Angus twins?'

He broke off as another member entered the lounge and stood up to speak with him at the door.

'What's happening, Liz?' Bethany whispered.

'Some prayers are getting answered and some prison doors are being opened.'

'You could simply ask them to leave the doors open and turn a blind eye as we pass.'

'They have lives that are dear to them too.'

The tension heightened as the morning progressed. In the conference theatre Keast felt increasingly wary, while the delegates had become visibly on edge and Sandy Angus was fidgeting with repressed alarm. Elsewhere in Neptune House the air buzzed with the feeling of dynamic change, of revelations of truth and the spring-cleaning of minds and motives. The tension peaked shortly before midday, when Pete and Charles walked purposefully back into the C.C.T.V. lounge.

'Mrs Graham, the members of P.S.I. have sent us to ask you to interrupt the conference,' Pete announced.

Bethany looked at her friend with marked astonishment which grew even greater when Liz shook her head.

'No, Mr Corrie: this is your society, not mine. If the conference needs to be interrupted, you do it.'

'We cannot stand up against those men down there, Madame,' Charles said: 'You already have; and despite all they have tried, you still do. We need your faith and resolve to inspire ours.'

'I will not go down there and turn around to find I'm on my own.'

'We promise you we will not do that,' Pete said.

Charles saw they were failing to persuade her. In desperation he tried a more emotive approach.

'Mme Graham, I implore you, not for ourselves but for the sake of all those poor young people who are still like Tim was until he met you. We could not save him, but you did. We cannot save P.S.I. but you can.'

His inference was deliberate, forcing her to abandon the modesty that made her avoid a situation because of its risk of personal glorification, for the more important cause of helping those who like herself and Tim and Alec's brother Kevin had lost much if not all of their lives to the control of a power greater than themselves called addiction, and through them their families and friends whose lives had also been damaged or destroyed. She realised her humility was misplaced and nodded to accept the challenge.

'What is your plan?'

Pete quickly outlined the course of action decided by the members. Liz asked him some questions to clarify her own role in the members' protest. She found as she spoke that she could not understand the words she heard herself speaking. An intermittent dysphasia was attacking her whenever she tried to advance the plan. Pete saw her increasingly concerned expression and asked her what was wrong.

'When I try to express myself, I seem to be saying a lot of nonsense,' she said, even more confused because she could understand herself perfectly that time.

'It does not sound like nonsense to me,' Charles said. 'Tell me, has anyone from P.S.I. hypnotised you?'

'Mr Keast did, last night.'

Charles nodded in understanding.

'I think he has tried to prevent you from carrying out the prophesies - he has placed a hypnotic block in your mind to distract you whenever you attempt an action against him. I can undo it, if you will permit me - it will require you briefly to go under again.'

Liz looked at Charles, weighing up whether she trusted him enough to submit. The decision was made when she realised that if she did not, the problem might never go away. She followed his instructions and relaxed back in her chair to concentrate on a sparkling cut glass pendant he swung gently in front of her eyes.

A few minutes later Liz took the lift with a party of seven members down to the theatre in the basement, while Bethany stayed with Tim in the lounge to watch events through the C.C.T.V. system. A crowd of members had gathered at the basement lift doors to welcome their rebel leader.

When Liz emerged from the lift, a long-haired woman dressed in flowing maroon robes stepped forward out of the waiting crowd, her henna-tattooed hands extended in welcome. She recalled the vision in her seance eight months before and embraced her.

'Yes. This is the one,' she said.

The crowd of members gathered round and greeted Liz in solidarity and reassurance. After confirming tactics, the advance party streamed in through the auditorium doors with Pete and Charles at their head, while Liz waited in the wings preparing to make her entrance.

The conference audience looked round in surprise. Speculative talk filled the theatre as more members crowded in along the walls of the tiered auditorium. The commotion threw the delegates off balance: some began to tidy their papers. Keast observed the disturbance in grim silence. His calculating eyes glowered at Pete as the under-manager raised his arms to quieten the audience, no longer daunted by the chairman's power.

'Chairman, delegates,' Pete shouted above the crowd, 'forgive us this interruption, but the members have decided Mrs Graham should have a chance to speak.'

The doors opened again and Liz entered. She paused at the top of the steps in serene confidence, willing the crowd to return to order. The voices hushed; those with seats sat back down; those in the aisle moved aside for her to pass. She descended ten steps and spoke, projecting her voice to fill the theatre with the same power she used when reading a lesson in Father Jay's chapel.

'Please accept my apologies, Chairman, Delegates: I didn't seek to make this disruption, but was asked to.'

She glanced upwards, suddenly aware that the air was filled with flying creatures like brightly coloured gargoyles come to life. Red and green and purple and gold, they circled high and dropped like stones to dive bomb her yet did not touch her. Were they really there, she wondered, or were they another manifestation of Keast's attempts to stop her deposing him? She signed herself with the rosy cross to shield herself and tried to ignore them as she continued her graceful descent to the stage.

When she reached the rostrum, she sheathed herself in the blue-edged white light of divine protection to make herself impervious to the evil being generated from its centre on the stage. The audience in the packed auditorium beyond the semicircle of antagonistic delegates seemed on balance to be supportive of her. Up in the windowed projection box above the back wall the technician raised a hand to signal her to begin. She handed the occasion over to her Higher Power, consciously opened her mind to divine inspiration and started to speak.

'*If a house is divided against itself, that house will not be able to stand*: Mark chapter 3 verse 25. I'm sure you all know the saying, even if you don't pick up a Bible from one year to the next. We all know the meaning, too, but we don't always live by it - I may quote it to coax loyalty from my friend; but am I so quick to remember it when I face indecision? Yes, indecision is also the product of a house divided against itself. And so is a person who wilfully continues to take an action or a substance which they know to be damaging. So why are you letting this happen here?'

She paused to let the audience consider her rhetorical question and took a sip from a glass of water in front of her on the rostrum. Keast and the delegates were giving her their complete attention, relieved to find their challenger was only delivering a sermon as it gave them ample leeway for counterattack. The chairman saw her look up into the air at something that was not there and realised that though his measures to distract her were working, they were failing to stop her. She dropped her gaze again, took out the small tin Tim had given her and continued to speak.

'The key factor of the psychic experience is the unity of humankind with itself, within creation and eternity. So why do you send even your most gifted children to oblivion? For the shortcut to inspired vision which you market in these pretty little tins, is a shortcut only to the grave and eternal non-being. It actually prevents the user from being able to reach that higher plane, that plane which anyone can reach with a bit of discipline and effort. You drown your brightest hopes at birth with this; and no amount of political lobbying and stylish literature and clever advertising can make up for the waste of so much new talent. So why do you do it?'

She put the tin back in her pocket and took another sip of water, sensing that something was trying hard to drain her spiritual power. She mirrored the force back upon itself and made the perpetrator Andropoulos recoil with the stab of a brief but searing headache. Around her the gaudy winged creatures crowded the stage but their malevolence could not touch her through her surrounding blue-edged white halo of divine protection. She spoke on.

'Well, for a start I discovered that more than half of you do not try to waste your psychic babes and really do believe in this society's charter - an interesting find in a democratically based corporate body. For the more than half who do try to develop psychic talent and promote psychic issues, are greatly hampered by the policy decisions of their co-opted delegates and representatives. And the death toll is chilling: four in Beirut, two in London, and one in Paris in the last six months alone; and that doesn't include all those who chose eternal oblivion for themselves either - how many more would they add to the number? Is that what this society set out twenty years ago to do? Is that what you all joined to do, and pay your subscriptions to fund your society and its representatives to do? Or is the democratic wish of this society really something quite different to what its chairman and delegates have been telling us all this morning?'

Keast looked up sharply, drawing Liz' attention upwards too. Both were startled to see Alec standing at the projection box window with the technician, looking down at them. Liz saw through Alec's stiff bearing to the betrayal he felt, having come to her rescue only to find her speaking from the conference rostrum like one of the P.S.I. delegates. In the face of this real distraction, the gothic winged creatures around her disintegrated into brown clouds and blew away. She put Alec's distressed anger out of her mind and drew her speech to a close.

'Aye, the Lebanese delegate was right when he said that

you must start now with some vast rethinking. It should start in this room, by the body of P.S.I., not its dubious delegates; with the correct procedural election of the chairman and delegates for the coming year, to see whether the members want new spokesmen to replace the old. And it should not stop until all the drug merchants and the murderers are thrown out on the streets, into the gutters where they belong. You must learn! If you want the house to stand...'

Terry screamed as a knife flashed through the air. Liz tried to duck behind the shelter of the rostrum but moved too late. The blade thudded into her left arm. She cried out in pain and fell to the floor.

The sudden attack stunned everyone in the theatre. For a moment the crowd hesitated, and then began to rise in dawning fury at the deed all had witnessed. The enraged knife-thrower Sandy Angus turned to face them and backed off, realising too late the folly of his act. He saw Alec through the projection room window and blanched. Before anyone thought to stop him, he took flight through the nearest stage door.

The other delegates abandoned the stage after him, fearing the horrified crowd would see little difference between him and them after Liz's speech. Keast fled the theatre with them, escaping only seconds before the mob began to move.

Terry ran to Liz and cried out to see her blood smearing the rostrum and pooling on the floor. As she shouted for a doctor the crowd's shock gave way to pure hatred. The members rose up *en masse* to chase after the men who had taken flight. Pandemonium filled the theatre. The conference broke up in chaos.

2 : 16

Alec's immediate reaction was to destroy Sandy Angus for stabbing his wife: he ran from the projection box in stony-faced determination to do the greatest damage he possibly could. Philip took over control of their rescue party, sending Sam to save Liz from the melee in the theatre and Theo to find Hendrik Gerber. He hurried out after them to look for Keast.

Sam found Liz sitting on the theatre floor leaning weakly against the rostrum while a young doctor applied a tourniquet to her arm to stop the bleeding. Bethany was sitting with her having come straight down from the C.C.T.V. lounge in the confusion to help her friend. At the doctor's request Sam carried Liz to a quieter room nearby where he could treat the knife wound.

The chaos in the rest of the building hindered Alec and Philip while helping the fleeing chairman and delegates escape. The brothers ran out into the rear car park behind Neptune House and watched in frustration as the last of seven cars accelerated away.

They ran back inside the building. Philip sprinted up the staircase to the first floor to check the offices in case one of Keast's team had been left behind. Alec called a lift to go down to the basement and his wife. When the lift door slid open in front of him, Terry Carter emerged. She froze but quickly recovered, wary of this man whose thirst for vengeance had stopped him from first rushing to his wife's side the way her friend Bethany had done.

'Ah, Dr Graham, I believe.'

She seemed pleased to meet him but for the slightly higher pitch to her voice.

'Miss Carter. Is my wife all right?'

'She'll live. The knife hit her in the arm, just below the left shoulder. A doctor's stitching up the wound.'

Terry guided Alec into the deserted post room behind the front hall reception desk to ensure no-one would see them together, giving him an unexpected opportunity to question her in private. She thought quickly, seeking a way to change sides to save herself, and produced a C120 tape cassette from her pocket.

'You'll want this. It's the only copy.'

Alec took it warily. The cassette bore the initials EG and the previous day's date, 16/8/77. 'This is, what, an interview?'

She shook her head. 'Jon drugged her and then hypnotised her. She tried everything she could to stop him, but she was helpless in his power.'

'So she did betray me.' His voice was flat and bitter.

'It wasn't her fault - she was only trying to help Bethany. That's how Jon arranged it - he knew that was the only way to get her. Not that she told him much he didn't already know. He wasn't really after information anyway - he was only trying to stop her overthrowing the leaders of P.S.I.'

'Liz, overthrow P.S.I.? Surely he didn't believe that!' Alec saw Terry's scornful look and explained, 'My wife is very lovely: I would say the nicest person I have ever known. But no-one would ever take her that seriously.'

'You say that, when you saw what just happened? Why do you think Jon sent me to befriend her?'

'He did it to use her to get at me - I was getting too close.'

Terry shook her head in disbelief at his arrogance.

'How wrong you are. Six months ago, a German Tarot diviner warned Jon a young woman would depose the leaders of P.S.I. and four people would die. A seer confirmed his reading soon after - she said she looked like a painted doll and would take all Jon held dear. Then a planchette seance spelled out the name Elizabeth Graham. Well, we looked for her but we couldn't find her, because she didn't yet exist. Then Pierre Eve suggested she might be the young woman you'd just met. So Jon sent me to befriend her through Bethany, hoping to avert the danger and the deaths by stopping her. You really played into his hands by leaving her in the dark.'

Alec turned aside, unable to assimilate this humbling assessment of his own power and influence. Instead, he ignored it as another example of his opponents' tactics of misinformation.

'Nonsense. He knew I was getting too close to him through Andrew Ferry and had the actor silenced.'

'No, Dr Graham. Jon hadn't realised Andrew Ferry had any connection with you - Ferry was a well-trained psychic long before he joined P.S.I. He died because the Angus twins found out he'd betrayed them to the police, no more. Then Marner went in to deal with any loose ends and found your name among the actor's personal effects. So Marner interviewed you, and then your wife; and finally we had found the painted doll. But the seer had failed to warn us that Liz is so much more than just a painted doll. It's her depth that enabled her to overthrow P.S.I.'

Alec heard the emotional edge to Terry's voice in her last statement and recalled overhearing a comment Bethany had made recently about Terry being gay. He found it much easier to believe that she was infatuatedly idolising Liz, than that her assessment of the situation was correct.

'So the seer's forecast was wrong,' he said.

'Quite the reverse: nearly all the forecast has been fulfilled. Two members are dead, Jon has disappeared, the delegates have fled and the members are up in arms. Your wife's speech has somehow placed this society in the palm of her hand. When we reconvene the conference after all the fuss has died down, the members will look for new leaders, and the first person they elect will, I'm sure, be her.'

A greedy glow washed over Alec as he saw the chance to take over an important part of Keast's empire through his wife. He pocketed the tape cassette with a swagger.

'And she will accept,' he promised.

'Will she? You only have my word she's even still alive.'

'Of course she's alive - you wouldn't be talking to me like this otherwise. I shall be waiting at Briarbank for your call.'

2 : 17

Alec stalked out of the post room into the hall. Philip emerged from the staircase and hurried over.

'Alec, it's time to go. Liz is in your car. She needs to go home.'

He propelled him out through the plate glass front doors onto the plaza. Alec told him about his meeting with Keast's secretary as they hurried over to the black Lincoln parked with the white Oldsmobile in a concealed entrance nearby. Alec got into the back of the Lincoln to sit beside Liz with Sam at the wheel and Bethany in the front passenger seat, while Philip and Theo stood watching Neptune House, still alert for danger. They then jumped into the Oldsmobile and the two cars drove off together onto Tottenham Court Road.

Liz lay in a corner of the back seat, propped up and with her eyes closed. Alec was taken aback to see how pale her face appeared beneath her makeup. In the front, Bethany looked very sheepish after Sam's recent criticism of her for causing all the trouble in the first place.

'How much damage?' Alec asked Bethany, drawing her attention to Liz.

'Just winged. Heaven knows how many stitches and no questions asked. How did you know to come for us here?'

'Process of elimination,' he lied, not wanting to admit to a pragmatist like Bethany that after all other avenues had failed, he and Philip had listened to Goldie's claim that Liz was in the arms of Neptune, and had used the relaxed security of the conference to infiltrate the building.

Alec watched his wife in concern during the journey home, holding her clammy right hand in his long fingers. Bethany was so surprised at his uncharacteristic show of sympathy she wondered what he was after.

'What happened to you both over the last twenty-four

hours?' he asked her. His manner seemed anxious rather than judgemental.

'I'm not too sure: they kept us drugged up most of yesterday,' Bethany said. 'And I can't say I actually understand what happened today, either. One minute, Liz was telling her life story to a drug addict, the next a delegation came asking her to stop the conference.'

Liz's eyes flickered open. She had been feigning sleep while she tried to gauge Alec's reaction to her adventure and her presence on stage when he had first seen her at Neptune House.

'What I did was twelve-step a young man who wanted to get better: I invoked my Higher Power and helped him evict his spirit familiar,' she said tiredly. 'When the other members saw the change in him, they asked me to do the same for their society.'

'Liz, you're awake!' Alec cried in joy.

He gave her an encouraging smile and fondly kissed her right hand.

'How did they treat you?' he asked in afterthought.

'Today, very well, because they thought we couldn't remember anything of yesterday,' Liz replied; 'But yesterday, very badly: I didn't eat for over twenty-four hours.'

She launched into a dispirited and disjointed description of all she could remember of her time at P.S.I., while Bethany regarded her with increasing astonishment.

'How can you remember all that, when they gave you twice as much cocktail powder as me?'

Liz smiled wanly. 'There are some advantages to being psychic.'

The two limousines turned into the Briarbank drive. Goldie came out to meet them. Alec asked her to take charge of the freed hostages and took Philip with him to the study to listen to the tape Terry had given him. Goldie sent Bethany off to her mother's care at nearby Ainhurst for the night, and placed Liz in the housekeeper's charge to ensure she had a meal and went to bed to sleep without disturbance until she woke naturally. Goldie then joined Alec and Philip in the study.

The air in the mellow book-lined room was crackling with anger. Philip was struggling to reason with Alec as he sat at the leather-topped desk viciously defacing a photograph of Keast with a letter opener. Goldie realised from what she could hear of the tape playing in the background that Alec was reacting to what he was imagining from the sounds on the tape rather than what had actually happened. She drew up a chair beside him and put her arm around his shoulders to comfort him, not deflected by his first involuntary flinch from her as he strove to remain aloof in his resentment.

'Your time comes soon, Alec. We have Liz back - it has not all gone his way,' she reassured him.

'And we have to listen to the rest of the tape to find out how much damage has been done to us,' Philip said.

Patiently they reasoned with Alec until he could listen to the recording objectively again. After the playback had ended, they discussed its implications. Goldie and Philip persuaded Alec never to tell Liz of the tape's existence or mention her interrogation by Keast again.

Several hours later, Terry phoned from P.S.I. to invite Liz to take Keast's place at P.S.I. Goldie snatched up the phone before Alec could reach it, and was not surprised to hear P.S.I.'s offer. Because she feared Alec and Philip would place undue pressure on Liz to accept, she arranged for the secretary to visit Briarbank later that day with the invitation in writing and with supporting information.

Terry arrived shortly before dinner. Alec and Philip interviewed her in the study while she waited for Liz, to find out what had happened at P.S.I.'s reconvened conference. She refused to comment until Liz was present.

When Liz finally appeared Goldie intercepted her in the hall and directed her to the lounge. Goldie then retrieved Terry from the study and ordered Alec and Philip to join them only if they said and did nothing to interrupt. The two men knew not to disobey their mother when so determined and could only watch as she completely changed their plans for the meeting.

Goldie sat down with Terry on the lounge sofa, placing herself between her and Liz, who was reclining listlessly in an armchair. With a smile to them both she settled down to observe too unless she saw Liz being pushed too far. Alec and Philip took their places where she had stipulated, outside the intimate circle, sitting on chairs by the wall where the two young women could not see them.

'How are you feeling now, Liz?' Terry enquired respectfully, hesitant in front of the critical audience behind her.

'I'm on the mend. Is P.S.I.?'

'I think so, now. The truth's just starting to come out from the branches, what Jon and the delegates had really been up to behind the scenes. The members are horrified - they still wouldn't believe it if they hadn't seen you get knifed.'

'Didn't they have any idea at all, what was going on?'

'Most of them, no. Most members aren't interested in the politics and the finances of P.S.I.: they pay their dues and read the newsletters and leave us to get on with our jobs. Those who did know were either Jon's men or not members for long. And you were right about the co-option: none of the delegates had contested their places in an election. Jon always arranged it so that no-one stood against them, and Jon's judgement was always accepted. After all, he did found the society twenty years ago, so it was natural to believe he always had P.S.I.'s best interests at heart.'

Terry paused to reorder her thoughts. Liz sensed her regret and assumed she felt upset by the dramatic changes taking place around her. Their three observers suspected the secretary's emotional conflict related rather to the people involved in the change. Terry smiled uncertainly at Liz and continued.

'The members followed the advice you gave in your speech, Liz. This afternoon they held elections according to the procedure laid down in our articles of incorporation, and they've chosen new representatives to take the places of the old. The person they elected to be the new chairman is you, if you are willing.' She opened her handbag and took out an envelope. 'Here is their formal invitation. They would appreciate your decision as soon as possible.'

Liz read the letter in astonishment. The invitation was the last thing she had expected from P.S.I. after all the trouble she had caused there. She looked back at Alec, imagining how he would feel about her taking office there when he had felt betrayed just to see her speaking from the rostrum at the conference. She was about to turn down the offer when Goldie intervened.

'Miss Carter, after all Liz has been through, your members are unfair to expect her to decide so soon. We need to discuss this as a family too. I suggest we all visit your society tomorrow, if Liz is well enough. Then we can all see what saying "yes" really means.'

'Of course, Mrs King: I shall warn the delegates and make the necessary arrangements.'

Terry stood up, disappointed, and turned to make one last more impassioned plea.

'Before I go, I would just like to say this. Liz, you know what you want for the world. If you accept, that is what you'll be working towards: the unity of humankind in the psychic experience you described in your speech. Don't deceive yourself that you aren't qualified for office. Experience you can get; the way you addressed the conference, and the way you healed Tim tell us you have the resources to cope. After everything collapsed around us at P.S.I., who else can we possibly trust besides you, the one who risked life itself with no thought of personal gain, just to help us get back on the right track.'

'Miss Carter, that is enough for tonight. Please leave the papers here for Liz to look through if she wants,' Goldie ordered.

Terry obediently put her papers down on the coffee table, less confident about the outcome after Goldie's firm dismissal. She thanked them for their time, said goodbye to Liz and left. As soon as she had gone, Alec and Philip moved into chairs closer to Liz to urge her to accept. Goldie returned from the hall and silenced them with a fierce look.

'I think it is right for Liz to ask for time to consider the offer,' she said, ignoring the fact that she was the one who had brokered this. 'Naturally Liz's first thought after all she goes through is to say no. I say it is a family matter to decide, for I know you both do not want Liz to say no.'

Liz looked up at Alec in surprise. 'Is that true?'

Alec muttered a non-committal answer which made her check to sense his true opinion. He felt annoyed at her caution and saw her acceptance as his personal victory over Keast which he could also use to his advantage in business. She recoiled from the bitter taste of his calculating, greedy vengeance and turned to Philip, only to find in him the equally bitter taste of future advantage. Goldie sensed her dismay and patted her right hand to reassure her.

'I think you are right to take time over this, Liz. All sides must be happy with the decision; but if it is not what you want for yourself, then soon no side will be happy with your decision. You are the one to live the life you choose - none of us can do that for you.'

Liz thanked her for her support and wondered what to decide for the best.

2 : 18

Liz returned to Neptune House after lunch the next day, travelling with Alec in the rear of the Lincoln while Sam drove with Philip beside him in the front. When the car drew up by the paved plaza outside Neptune House, Philip jumped out and warily kept watch for trouble as he opened the rear door for Liz and Alec to alight. Liz stepped out into the sunshine and gazed up at the seven-storey office block which P.S.I. had inherited through the bequest of a late member. She was wearing a loose white dolman-sleeved dress to conceal her bandaged left arm without over-dressing for the oppressively hot summer day. She stepped aside for her husband to alight and started nervously as a bus hurtled past inches away from the limousine.

A powder blue Jaguar flew out of a side turning and raced past them after the bus. Three shots rang out. Philip threw Liz to the ground to shield her with his body while Alec and Sam returned the fire from the shelter of the limousine. Their first shot went wide, their second hit a front tyre, their third hit the driver, Doug Angus. The Jaguar spun out of control and broad-sided a lamp post. A laden wagon behind tried to brake but its wheels locked. It skidded on and crushed the side of the car, killing the rear seat passenger, Rolf Krueger.

A momentary stillness froze the scene. Then the front passenger door of the Jaguar swung open. Sandy Angus fell out onto the pavement, his face bleeding, a gun falling from his hand.

Alec nodded to Sam to cover him and cautiously moved out of the safety of the Lincoln to check the Jaguar, his revolver held forward in both hands ready to fire. Philip used his movement as a cover to bundle Liz back into the limousine. She watched in horror as Alec straightened up and aimed his revolver at Sandy Angus' head. Sandy's right hand scrabbled on the pavement to reach his own gun lying a few inches from his fingertips. Alec kicked the weapon well out of his way.

'This one's for my wife!'

'Don't shoot!' Liz screamed.

Alec paused, distracted, his concentration broken. A short distance away a police siren started to wail.

'I didn't stab your wife. That was Sandy,' Angus pleaded desperately.

'Tell that to the court, Sandy!' Alec sneered. But the moment of temptation had passed: he uncocked his gun and re-holstered it.

Philip bundled Liz back out of the limousine and across the forecourt into Neptune House, leaving Alec and Sam to keep trouble and the police at bay.

Several P.S.I. members had gathered in the foyer to welcome Liz. They were horrified by what they had just witnessed through the plate glass entrance doors. To make her forget the latest attempt on her life, they gave her a whirlwind tour of the society, full of introductions. The deluge of information so overwhelmed her that after two hours of it she requested time alone to reflect. Terry swiftly altered schedules and arranged for her to have a twenty minute break in the basement theatre, promising that even Alec and Philip would be kept out.

Liz entered the theatre through the door at the back of the auditorium as she had done at the conference. The stage had been cleaned since the melee of the previous day, but the set was still in place: the horseshoe table for the fourteen delegates, the speaker's rostrum and the desk for the chairman and secretary. Liz stepped slowly down the tiers towards the stage, replaying the events and the reactions of those present. She recalled standing at the rostrum to deliver her extempore speech, and wondered again whether the strange winged creatures around her had really been there, made visible by Keast's hypnosis, or if they were just hallucinations. She moved along the horseshoe table remembering the delegates responses: Rolf Krueger's intolerance, Hendrik Gerber's calculative dismay, Phineas Andropoulos' attempts to sabotage her, Sandy Angus' barely controlled anger. She sat down in Angus's place at the end of the table and reviewed the decision she had to make, feeling far more lonely and insecure now than at that moment when he had thrown his knife at her to kill.

She dearly wanted to accept the chair but questioned her

ability to fill the office with the impartiality it required when the people around her were pressurising her to accept because they hoped to gain through her. Within the society she sensed hidden divisions between the different psychic disciplines which could prove difficult to reconcile. P.S.I.'s profitable commercial interests sought capital reinvestment, despite the society's need to redirect their profits into less profitable member services such as training and information as these would no longer be funded by drug trafficking. If she could not broker compromise or find other sources of funding, she might need to reduce services and consider staff redundancies which would not make her popular as a newcomer. She also feared malice and violence would re-emerge in the society even though the criminals had gone. The role the society had invited her to accept would not be an easy one.

She longed to discuss the problem with Alec, but could not trust his advice when he wanted her to accept because of the benefits he envisaged from linking his business interests with P.S.I.'s overseas network. Her only other possible advisers, Father Jay and Harry Simms, had been unavailable when she had phoned them: the priest was still busy with Tim, and the bookseller was away all day at a sale in Lincoln.

Tears of loneliness pricked her eyes. Impatiently she wiped them away with the back of her hand, too lost in thought to hear the movement of the auditorium door behind her or sense the threat that had just entered.

'What, tears; on this your day of victory?' mocked Jonathan Keast, disconcerted to witness such unexpected vulnerability in his rival. This was not the woman he had come to remove: that was a brash gold-digger who could not wait for the ink to dry on the contract. He re-holstered his gun and stepped softly down the auditorium steps towards the stage.

'They say power corrupts, but they never mention the corrupting influence of those around the person in power. It is so hard to decide regardless of what they want.'

Her remark told him she had not yet identified him beyond sensing he was someone who could understand her dilemma. Her vulnerability enticed him. There were other ways of exacting revenge besides killing, he thought, recalling her repressed physical attraction for him. As a practising Christian and the wife of his adversary she was not only desirable but would make a significant conquest. He crossed the stage to the Greek delegate's place and leaned against the horseshoe table where she would have to see him if she looked up.

'No person is innocent who is weak enough to let others persuade him into corruption.'

She hardly heard him in her impatience at her own inability to see beyond the facade of the day.

'Who dealt Card XV, the Devil, in this spread?' she demanded, looking up with a toss of her head. Her eyes fixed on his. She faltered and paled to discover just who was counselling her.

'Whoever may interpret the reading, you are the one who shuffled the pack.'

He contemplated her expression, feeling the movement of her confused emotions over his desire for her. Even in her vulnerability she had some force which he needed but could not identify. He began to probe for the weaknesses that would let him break through her guard.

'You are concerned about your husband?'

She nodded. His question helped her crystallise her thoughts and work through the issues. She was angry with Alec for feeling justified to murder Sandy Angus in cold blood in the street because the man had attacked her in anger at the conference. She disapproved of her husband for still playing playground games of good and evil, but disapproved with concern because he now played with live ammunition and mortal men. And his assumption that through her P.S.I. was about to become a part of his business empire troubled her, because she knew that if she took office she would have to defy and even deny him at last.

'Lord, give him eyes to see,' she whispered, but meant a mind to understand.

Her prayer cut through to the heart of Keast's jealousy, stabbing him with regret that fate had chosen so late in his career to give such a woman to his foe. He strove to overcome his self-betrayal with an increased determination to seduce her from Alec.

'You are his eyes,' he said.

His comment helped her see how God had placed her and Alec together for Alec to become less worldly while she became more so; but while her husband refused to place her before his own interests, her influence on him would fail. Her loneliness through Alec's lack of emotional support, related directly back to the intense loneliness she had felt in her teens which she had hoped to escape in the close bond of marriage. She was responding to her adversary's sympathy because of her hunger for emotional understanding, recognising that he too had known loneliness and could identify with her.

He sensed her loneliness and found it tugging at his own. In his choices of early manhood, it had been easy to scorn companionship, when he had given in to material pressures and dedicated himself to a temporal existence alone; but at fifty-four that choice was no longer so palatable. He had willingly sacrificed much to build up P.S.I. as his living monument, only to have his sacrifices made worthless by this woman who could have been his daughter, when it was too late for him to change course. But if he could only steal her, he would win back the society through her too.

'I know P.S.I. wants you to take my place. Take it: you are the only person I could give it to.'

His admission of defeat startled her: she looked up into his face in surprise. He nodded with a smile of confirmation, pleased that she continued to watch him: it made it easier to manipulate her emotions enough to take control.

'You are right to look so surprised. I was the one who arranged for you to be gunned down in the street today. When I saw that plan fail, I took it upon myself to deal the fatal blow. Oh, the bitter temptation of revenge! You had taken my life work; I would take your life.'

He unholstered his revolver and placed it beside him to underline his words. She tensed involuntarily and pulled back from his dangerous unpredictability. Her attention was totally his.

'Don't worry, Liz: I won't use it on you now. I hadn't realised until I saw you here again, how much I've been deceiving myself about you. I've met many people in my lifetime, all outwardly different but beneath all so predictably the same. I saw the greed in myself and acknowledged it; I saw it in those who did not acknowledge it in themselves and despised them. At your age I chose to join their ranks rather than be a martyr for idealism: they deserve no pity for receiving the measure they give to others, and I have enjoyed doing well by them. But you? You are different: never before have I met anyone like you. You are like the person I chose in my youth not to be; but I was lost then in a world you should fortunately never know. I am not strong enough to reverse that decision, nor do I expect ever to be now: it's too late to change.'

Though his words had an aura of sincerity, Liz mistrusted them because she sensed he was not the sort to betray willingly the human frailty behind his mask of strength. She resisted the surge of pride which had welled up in response to his flattery, and determinedly focused on the impersonal.

'They say it's never too late to change. That's why this decision is so difficult. How would my involvement with P.S.I. change me, and change my husband; and do I really want those changes to happen?'

'No-one can stand still in time, Liz: if you deny yourself the risk of change you will regress - failing to embrace experience brings only atrophy and decay. Time will change me, I know - it will make me bitter. Yes, I will remember you as you sit here now; but your compassion will become contempt, the sympathy in your face will mask self-interest, your honesty an act to hide your hatred. Self-interest, hatred and contempt are all I know, so naturally time will change my memory of you into someone like everyone else. And in a few years' time I will return to depose the cunning upstart whose scheming ways stole my life work from me. If you have stood still or changed for the worse, I shall have no conscience about exacting my revenge and ridding P.S.I. of another charlatan. But if experience matures your faith, I would do well to give up before I begin, for I cannot harm a saint.'

He re-holstered his gun and stood up to gaze thoughtfully at the chairman's desk, suspecting that before the decade had ended, he would be dead. She heard a distant whisper of his fear through the stone wall he had built around his emotions and reached out to him across the dark void separating them in spirit.

'You are lonely too, Jon, aren't you?'

He turned to look back at her, a flicker of a smile touching the corners of his mouth. At last she was responding to him of her own accord. His head instinctively lifted higher as he went in for the emotional kill.

'I am far less lonely than you will be, Liz; for at least I still have friends around me like Hendrik who understand the pleasures and the pain. No-one can reach as high as you.'

He turned as if to go, leaving unsaid his willingness to try to reach her; but she heard his tacit offer and quickly spoke without thinking to make him stay.

'I would expect you back in twelve months: if you don't return within five years, I'll wonder what kept you. So rest assured I'll be prepared. And thanks, Jon: you've helped me see what I've got to do.'

'If I have done that, I have lost my advantage. Perhaps that will help offset the debt I owe you for my lack of consideration before today.'

He crossed the stage to her place at the horseshoe table and stood before her to admire the prize he was moving in to take. Her beautiful heart-shaped face was pale behind her perfect make-up. Not one strand of black hair was out of place in her stylish coiffure, and her piquant scent filled his senses with a bitter-sweet perfume.

'I will remember you as you sit here,' he promised.

Their eyes met. He sat down before her on the edge of the table and leaned closer. Her lips parted slightly in expectation. He placed his right hand on her left shoulder and drew her towards him.

Suddenly she leapt back, the stab of pain in the injured arm from the chill authoritarian grasp of his hand warning her of the danger he was really luring her into. For one who felt bound by her marriage vows, she knew his kiss was the kiss of death, his possession adultery, his sympathy the devil's temptation to lead her into sin.

He saw at once that the chance had gone and he had failed. This precious jewel could not be snatched: he would need to do a lot more planning to ensure she did not foil his next attempt. He broke away and quit the theatre before she sounded the alarm and his failure with her also got him caught.

For a few minutes Liz stood there analysing the temptation which had almost undermined her integrity. From past experience she knew that overcoming a stiff temptation usually heralded an important spiritual advance. She crossed the stage and sat down in the chairman's position. In front of her the delegates' places and the tiers of seats filled with a vision of crowds of people shining with joy at her presence there. All too soon the envisioned crowd thinned until no-one was there.

The whisper of a door brought Liz back to the present. She watched Terry enter the auditorium with Alec, Pete Corrie and Charles Lafayette, and realised Terry must have been responsible for Keast's safe passage through Neptune House to meet her in the theatre. She also knew that through that conversation Keast had shattered a fragile lie on which her life had recently balanced, through his showing her the emotional attention Alec could not give. She understood why Goldie had told her she was the only one to live her life, and no longer saw any reason to refuse the position she wanted so much, solely because she doubted the motives of all the other people who also wanted her to say yes.

Liz looked powerfully up from the chairman's seat, her expression serene. She announced, 'I have decided to accept.'

THE END